Jill Da...

Jill Dawson was born in 1962 in Durham and grew up in Yorkshire. She read American Studies at Nottingham University and after graduating moved to London where she worked in a variety of temporary jobs. In 1984, she won a poetry and a *City Limits* short story competition and from then on focused on writing, becoming a Writer in Residence in Doncaster at the age of twenty-five and winning the Eric Gregory Award for Poetry in 1992. *Trick of the Light* is her first novel, but she is also the author of the non-fiction book *How Do I Look?*, and editor of *The Virago Book of Wicked Verse* and *The Virago Book of Love Letters*. She lives with her young son in Hackney.

SCEPTRE

# Trick
# of the
# Light

## JILL DAWSON

**SCEPTRE**

Extract on pages 90–91 is from 'The Ballad of Jed Clampett'
by Paul Henning. © 1962 Carolintone Music, Inc. Renewed.
Used by permission. All rights reserved.
Extract from *The Chemehuevis*, Carobeth Laird,
Malki Museum Press, 1976.

First published in 1996 by Hodder and Stoughton
A division of Hodder Headline PLC
A Sceptre Paperback

10 9 8 7 6 5 4 3 2 1

British Library Cataloguing in Publication Data

Dawson, Jill
   A trick of the light
   1. English fiction – 20th century
   I. Title
   923.9'14


ISBN 0 340 65383 3

Typeset by Palimpsest Book Production Limited,
Polmont, Stirlingshire
Printed and bound in Great Britain by
Cox and Wyman Ltd, Reading, Berkshire

Hodder and Stoughton
A division of Hodder Headline PLC
338 Euston Road
London NW1 3BH

For Lewis Dawson, with love

# ACKNOWLEDGMENTS

I am indebted to Jane Rogers for careful reading of this manuscript and for the generosity of her tutoring and advice. Also to those on the MA fiction course at Sheffield Hallam University for comments and encouragement. I'd also like to thank the following people: Stewart Read for introducing me to the landscape described here and for sharing it with me; Sarah Leigh for her hard work on my behalf; Carole Welch for sensitive editing; Robert Miles for his belief in me; Jim Pollard for friendship and great plot discussions; and Joanna Ryan for everything.

'Coyote embodies all the human traits: laziness and patient industry or frantic exertion; foolishness and skilful planning; selfishness and concern for others . . . he is the incomplete and the imperfect . . . Coyote has fun and it's fun to hear about him and his exploits. What he lacks in dignity he makes up in sheer exuberance.'

Carobeth Laird, *The Chemehuevis*

## 1

I take an axe to Mick's head. I creep up behind him, his blond hair is yellow in the sun, like a halo, his brown back wet with sweat. Or maybe it isn't an axe, but some other tool, a simple mallet, easier for me to manage than an axe. He doesn't hear me, my feet in trainers are silent on the grass, my glasses are slipping down my nose but I can't free a hand to push them up again, both arms are raised, elbows pointing to the sun, with the mallet – no, definitely an axe, a mallet is way, way too small – suspended behind me, now curving up in an arc. The wonderful moment when gravity, force, time has taken over, when I don't have to think about what I'm doing, don't have to imagine the crunch of metal on skull, the chunky cut it would make, not clean but messy, the bone and blood and flesh munched up together. And then I wake up.

My hot sticky cheek is pressed up against the window of the truck. There is a smell of cooped-up bodies, of warm, smoky plastic and orange peel. I shift position and in the first two seconds have no idea where I am. Which car, which country, which journey. My neck is aching, my right thigh has gone dead from resting all my weight on it. I realise this when Mick reaches across the baby strapped in the child-seat between us, grins at me and gives my alive thigh a squeeze, then flexes his fingers on the steering wheel.

'All right, doll? Everybody doing fine?' He says, in his compère voice, an announcer, introducing the next act, keeping the audience happy. It's a reference to my short-lived career as a singer, if career is the word for a couple of years of pub gigs. I smile back at him, and twist around in my seat to check on Frances. She's sleeping, red T-shirt wrinkled over her fat belly, sweaty curls sticking to her head. A giant packet of Huggies is wedged on the floor, in the place where my feet should rest.

'Where are we?' I ask, trying my best to stretch without jogging Frances or dislodging the Huggies.

'Welcome to the United States of America, Land of the Freeway,' Mick says. This time it's his American voice, his TV chat-show host. I yawn, grin, take my glasses off and wipe them on my T-shirt. Through my smeary window is a wide expanse of lake, blue as a spearmint, and the road has narrowed, is rising.

'Don't be silly, I mean, where are we?'

'Diablo Dam,' Mick says. 'You've been asleep since Sedro Woolley.'

'I wasn't asleep.'

'Whatever. This is the North Cascades Highway. You're missing all the views. And this baby' – he pats the dashboard, grinning again – 'is running like a dream. She's pulling fantastically, we're doing forty even with this load, and we're nearly eight thousand feet up . . .'

The truck, which I'm trying to remember to call a pick-up, is some rusty red thing, a Ford, I think. It reminds me of the toy ones my brothers had, with their empty flat backs, only our pick-up isn't empty; what Mick calls the 'bed' (a black plastic tray, segmented, like a giant version of the inside of a cutlery drawer) is stuffed to the brim with planks of wood, a bath-tub (10 dollars from a thrift store, but I'm dubious, the edges look rusted and scratchy), a fold-up camping stove, a huge round water barrel, tied down with rope, a chair, a travel cot, a push-chair, four huge sheets of dirty glass wrapped in newspaper. Most of these have been picked up in the last week while me and Frances have been recovering from the flight and staying with Mick's brother Jon and his wife Carole, at Mount Vernon. Scouring the goodwill and thrift shops is fine by me, but the best bargains – Levi 501s in my size for a dime – Mick keeps telling me to leave behind. 'We need furniture Rita, you can get all that stuff later. Try and remember, we're here now for a *long time*. There's no rush to buy clothes, surely?'

But that's just the trouble. I can't remember. I can't shake off the holiday feeling, it's the newness, the hot weather, the shorts and T-shirts and ice-creams, the cases. It's the accents, the strange thin milk, the tanned square faces of Carole and Jon, the pale beers late in the evening, outside on the raised up wooden deck, the cedar-smell of the house, the mosquitoes. When I look inside my case, which I do frequently, at the thick wool sweaters, the carefully stashed dollars, the *Book of Western Forests* and *Ten Simple Solar Projects*, the twenty boxes of ten non-allergic condoms (I'm not sure if you can get them in the States, and Mick is very sensitive) then I start to remember, with a jolt. But that doesn't mean it sinks in.

'Are you going for good?' Nicola suddenly whispered, at Heathrow airport, her face in my hair, me bundled up to the gills with baby and buggy and baggage, trying to receive her goodbye hug. How could she have left it so late to ask? I'd been relying on her to ask, so that I could find out my answer.

'I don't know. What's there to come back for? I want to be with Mick,' I'd said, a damp, tearful remark – was that only a week ago? Jet-lag does something weird to your time, to your days, stretching them out then eating them up again, so that the lag is real, you feel it. There has been a lag somewhere, and surely that conversation happened in another lifetime?

Nicola waving tearily, a woman with a head of twig-like

dreadlocks, blue spotty leggings and a black bra top, dark and small through my blurry glasses as I pushed Frances across the shiny floor towards the Departure Lounge, is such a tiny remaining image. But that's all there is. No parents (Mum rang me the week before to wish me luck, and sent me the red T-shirt for Frances, I haven't heard from my Dad for years), no brothers (various excuses: Dan says he might come for a visit; Billy is broke; Tony's girlfriend is pregnant), no workmates (simple reason: no work). The absolute opposite of our arrival in Seattle, where Mick met us, at Sea-Tac airport, grinning and shining in his black leather jacket, twirling me off my feet and trying to kiss us both at the same time, with Frances squealing in my arms and Mick's scratchy blond stubble all over my face and neck.

'Wait 'til you see it Rita, wait 'til you see it. You're going to love it,' he was saying, ruffling Frances's head, knocking my bag off my shoulder.

This was not the moment to ask him to explain everything at once – I hadn't seen him for six weeks, the phone calls couldn't come anywhere close to this blue-eyed Mick, hot, coffee-smelling, laughing – the cabin, the land, the mountain, the area, I'd ask about that later. I'd done everything he asked: sent my paltry savings over, sorted out my visa, packed the Box (a plyboard contraption Mick made before he left), given the keys to the squat to Mick's friend Spider, phoned the Sea Removals company to send the Box over, and most of all, I'd got us here. Wrapped in Mick's giant bear-hug, I couldn't stop grinning.

Where here is, now that's another matter. I suppose at the moment we are high up – on the left there's a view of the lake and then the road climbs and there's a valley with pointy dark tips of trees, and my ears are popping, and Mick keeps saying 'Wow! Look down there!' There are neat, new road signs with names like 'Cut-Throat Pass' and 'Granite Creek' and other more worrying signs that say

'Road Closed in Winter' or 'Check Your Brakes'. And there are mountains, sometimes looming up beside us, sometimes appearing in the distance like peaks on a meringue, as we career around a bend.

Mick says he's glad the weather is so good, the planks of wood won't get wet, although there might be mist in the Methow Valley, and I say, remembering, that it's the first of June, Nicola's birthday. Then we both fall silent again. I've always had difficulty with big scenes; trees, mountains, snow, lakes, views, horizons. Give me a flower or a mushroom, a blade of grass, mud-pies and daisy chains, a spider's leg, a tadpole; that I can appreciate. Mick is the opposite. He's never at a loss for expressions of wonder – 'Fucking hell, Rita, look at that!' He likes the way things look from a distance. To me they are often vague, a blur. I have to be up close – with my glasses on – to see anything at all. The only thing I notice is the names, I like the names. Ruby Mountain. Ruby Creek. Rainy Pass. Silver Star Mountain.

'Loads of these places are called Ruby this or Silver that. Have you noticed?' I say.

'That's cos thar's gold in them thar hills. Or silver,' Mick says. This is a voice from a kids' TV programme, I can't remember which. I'm not sure if he's serious.

'We might even have some on our bit of land,' Mick says, but whatever else he was about to say gets interrupted. Frances wakes up and finding her nappy wet and her legs cramped and her skin hot and sweaty – she begins yelling.

## 2

After the Methow Valley is the town of Winthrop, a film set, a street lined with brand new wooden houses, a 'Genuine Wild West store', and a 'Saloon'. 'Touristy,' announces Mick, although he knows Frances is hungry, and drives on. Then there's another mountain pass – the Loup Loup, which I see nothing of because Frances is throwing things at the windscreen; her bottle, her Sindy, an orange, and I am preoccupied with attempts to anticipate, to catch things before they go, trying to wrestle them out of her hand without provoking too many squeals, which would disturb Mick.

'We're all hungry, we're all tired,' I say, ostensibly to Frances. 'Daddy will stop soon. He knows you need something to eat. Come on now. Have another piece of orange, hmm?'

In only six weeks Mick seems to have forgotten what it is like to be with Frances. At eighteen months, big for her age, loud and squawky, she's never been one to slip into the background. Apart from when she's sleeping, which is my favourite time of day, I can never switch off from Frances. It's amazing to me that Mick can.

We drive through a bigger town – Okanogan – which is tattier, not so new, but once again where the whole town, all the houses and shops seem to have been built on either side of one straight road, pretend houses, a cardboard town, there's nothing behind them. Old men here wear the same clothes as younger ones; they just pull their baggy jeans in with a belt, wear the peak on their baseball caps the right way round. We drive across a bridge, the Okanogan river – slowly: the driving speed in towns is something ridiculous like 25 mph. The next town is Omak but we're through that quickly. A sign claims Colville Indian reservation, but though I search for differences, there's nothing discernible, only a huge billboard on two long legs advertising bingo with a cut-out dancing horse next to it, and a another smaller one saying 'Tribal Elections: Vote Don Wattson'. Or Watt Donson. American names are always the wrong way round. Even Indian ones it seems.

We've joined a different highway now – Mick says 'Here we are at last, 97' – and even I can tell we're in an enormous valley, somewhere flat and low with fields which are pale honey in colour. We've lost all the pine trees, the mountains are a backdrop; now the road is wide, with houses dotted periodically. They all have horses and two or three cars, on the roadside there are billboards advertising the Omak Stampede (with the same picture of the dancing horse from the bingo ads) and sometimes there are rows of small round trees, fruit trees, propped up with wooden sticks. Frances has put her thumb in and is sucking noisily; I can tell from Mick's shifting and fidgeting and attempting to roll a cigarette, balancing the tin in his lap, that we will at least stop soon, that we're not far.

The town we stop in is called Sinkalip. It appears from nowhere, a sign saying 'Sinkalip Welcomes Careful Drivers'. One minute we're on the wide, wide road, with Mick singing 'I get my kicks, on Route Sixty-six!', on either side of us are huge fields (some of them full of this dry-looking grass, Mick says it's sage-brush; the locals gather it and sell it, but he doesn't know what for), mountains on the horizon, a little wooden church, a Used Tyre centre stuck out in the middle of nowhere; the next minute we're driving into town. Sinkalip is the kind of town where you can look down the main road and see its end from the beginning. The high street divides wooden-fronted shops, a gas station, a Mini-Mart, a Seven-Eleven, Hank's Hardware, and then in the distance, open road again, more mountains.

'God,' I say, 'Sinkalip is weird. Now I know what they mean in Westerns when they say a "one-horse town". It's so little! And all that space behind the buildings. Weird.' I'm starving. 'There's a caff, Mick, Aunt Pattie's Burger Stop. What about that?'

'Na. I stopped there before. Horrible chips and weak coffee. Look, there's "Joe Mason: Real Estate", that's where I bought the land. We'll have to call in there next week, get a proper map. Here's somewhere – what about this? The Round-Up Café?'

He parks right outside. No yellow lines, parking meters here – there's so much space, every road is wide enough for four lanes of traffic, although there are only two. Pick-ups are definitely the thing to be seen in, the more bashed up the better, and Mick loves the ones with giant wheels, he says he's going to buy a toy one, a shiny green Chevy. For Frances.

Heat hits us the minute we step out of the truck. Dry, breezeless heat – one hundred degrees of it. I wish I could wear sun-glasses but being so short-sighted I've never found any that I can actually see with. Frances has a pair, though, yellow with a bee over her nose. I pop them on her as I lift her out of the baby-seat.

The Round-Up Café is empty except for an old man wearing what Mick calls a 'hickory shirt' – a shirt that loggers wear in a thin, ticking material – sitting at the counter, chatting to the waitress. She refills his coffee before trotting over to our table.

'Hi now. Can I get you folks a high chair for the baby?'

She has a high blonde ponytail, the kind that swings when you walk, tight jeans and a spanking new Bryan Adams T-shirt. She sets down two glasses of water, two thick white coffee mugs and brings us the high chair. Once Frances is installed she gives her a flat balloon with I LOVE THE ROUND-UP CAFÉ on it.

As soon as we try to order she grins at us, coffee pot raised in one hand.

'Where you all from?'

I let Mick do the talking. He loves telling people. England. No we're not on holiday. We've bought a place up here. On Mount Coyote. Yes, we do know there's no electricity. Yes. Or water. Yes. Yes, in London. It was advertised in the paper. No not in London. Over here. Visiting my brother, he lives at Mount Vernon. No I'm not English, but Rita is. I have dual citizenship. Yes. Um. Bryan Adams is OK. Yeah – there is a problem with the IRA in London, but not as bad as you might think from the news . . . Yes, Frances is a doll, isn't she. Finally we get to order – two all-day special breakfasts and an extra plate for Frances – and flex our stiff legs under the table. The walls are decorated with guns and a couple of antlers, and some photographs of deer, framed in glass and made into clocks, with a greasy handwritten postcard beneath them. 'Any of these for sale. Ask Betty at counter.'

'Not far now,' Mick says, taking a breath between blowing up the balloon for Frances.

'How far?' I ask suspiciously.

'Oh, about eight miles at the most. Mount Coyote is the other side of town, past the orchards. And our place is about half way up the mountain, not at the top.'

'How on earth did you find it, the first time?'

'Well in the paper it just gave Sinkalip as a reference, and Joe Mason's number to phone. He told me to drive through town and take the first right straight after the sign for Goldtown. That's the bottom of the mountain. You'll see. It wasn't that difficult.'

He hands the balloon to Frances. Once again I have a stab of disbelief. Did we really do it, did we buy *some land* for God's sake, us? And some land in North-East Washington, miles from anywhere, half way up a bloody mountain? I'm exhausted, a headache has descended on me, every limb is aching from being cramped in the truck, Frances is batting the balloon on her head and squealing.

'Don't worry. Bout a ting,' says Mick, in his Rasta voice.

The waitress brings the all-day breakfasts.

'Your accents are real neat,' she says.

Leaving Sinkalip, the sage-brush fields change into orchards. Squat rows of trees, no sign of fruit. ('Washington Reds,' Mick says. 'All gloss and polish on the outside, watery crap on the inside.') Wooden props rest against the trees, empty crates beside each one. After the orchards come the workers' houses, and the Mexicans, hanging around the flimsy white boxes smoking, with little straggles of dark-eyed children playing outside, groups of skinny dogs and in one front yard, hens. Next to the box houses are sunflowers, nearly as tall as the houses, the tallest sunflowers I've ever seen. The sign for Goldtown ('Welcome to Goldtown. Goldtown says No to Drugs') comes up, and the turning on the right, and Mick takes it. Frances is too hot, squirming in her baby-seat, so I'm struggling to take her T-shirt off without undoing her strap.

There's no sign for Mount Coyote. I don't know why I expected one. There's no sign for our place either, Mick says, just a lot number. He's still raving about the price. Six thousand dollars. You can buy fuck-all in England for that.

The road we're on is bumpy, just a gravel track, dust flies up behind us and our heads jolt around on stalks. The fruit trees are replaced by pines again, first a few pines, then more pines. We're climbing and what we've just passed becomes a view; white houses and neat orchards, mountains in the distance. Strange birds strut and flap at the side of the road – little fat ones with curly question-marks above their heads – maybe they're quails, but I don't know if they have quails in this part of the world? In the sky I can see a huge bird, something impressive with gold and red on its tail – I don't want to sound silly so I daren't ask Mick if it's an eagle – and on the telegraph lines a whole host of birds, different sizes and shapes, lining up like a bus queue.

As we climb further in the struggling pick-up there are more pine trees and the telegraph lines disappear. The road we're on forks, and at the bottom of the fork is a row of about a dozen mailboxes, on their own, in the middle of nowhere.

'That's obviously as far as the mail man comes up,' Mick comments, taking the left fork.

Notices nailed on trees warn about forest fires and suggest that in the event of one Channel 6 should be used, to contact Lewis Roberts the fire officer. Or was that Robert Lewis?

We pass a couple of houses, well hidden behind the trees, but what glimpses I catch I study intently. One sign pinned on a tree says 'Mary and Rob's Place' (the fire officer? he has two large pick-ups outside his front door, but neither looks like a fire truck), the other cabin is called 'Nancy and Jim's Place'. Both houses are made of logs, Mary and Rob's is bigger and more open, Nancy and Jim have even more cars and bits of cars around, both houses seem real enough – what did I expect? – although surely they should be more *separate* or open, not growing out of the pines and bushes and cars like that? Suddenly Mick veers into the trees.

'This is our driveway,' he mutters, a cigarette between his teeth. He drives slowly, his shoulders tense.

I'm craning my neck to see. A long flattened-grass drive, scattered with pine cones, most of them crushed or broken in half – why is that? – and raggedly lined with trees, all of them, as far as I can see, pines of some sort. At the end of it, flanked by larger trees, a square house made of logs piled one upon the other, it might be a gingerbread house, or made from chocolate logs, if it weren't for the ugliness and irregularity. Grey peeling bark, flapping plastic roof, black windows like little gaping mouths.

Around the cabin is an assortment of junk; logs, pieces of rusty metal, broken toys, old clothes, beer cans. Grasses and shrubs grow up between them, everywhere small branches, twigs and tree-stumps cluster, and entangling themselves amongst them are large yellow flowers, giant daisies, their petals singed a dirty brown at the top.

'Here we are, ladies,' says Mick, switching off the engine.

Frances gives a loud squeal, and bashes her balloon at the dashboard. It pops.

# 3

I open the truck door and set a sleepy Frances down on the grass, giving her a gentle prod in the back and expecting her to go off like a clockwork toy. Instead she squats down, perfectly still. Something has caught her eye.

'Flower,' I tell her.

'That's heart-leaf arnica.' Mick stands, hands on hips, surveying. 'The yellow flowers – I looked them up in the book. They were everywhere when I first got here, I'm surprised they're dying so quickly.'

Arnica is what the homoeopath recommended, immediately after child-birth. For bruising and shock. It came in tiny white tablets, looked nothing like this straggly, over-sized yellow daisy. It was useless; I decide I hate the bloody stuff.

'Maybe we should call the cabin that, Arnica House,' Mick says cheerfully, hauling his rucksack from the back of the truck.

'Ar-nee-ca, ar-nee-ca' Frances is saying, she's learned a new word. I watch Mick unlock the padlock on the cabin door, amazed at the trouble he's gone to, when all four windows are nothing but huge holes; the edges dusty, dotted with bits of bark. It's sunny, it can't be six o'clock yet, but inside the cabin is dark and surprisingly cold. It feels like a barn, high-roofed, bits of stuffing peeping out from between the logs and scattering the floor, pieces of wood and logs piled in one corner, a brush and bucket in the other. There is a lumpy blue mattress, with blankets thrown on it, and against the back wall a sofa, mud-coloured. I plonk myself down on it, ask 'Did you buy it?' and we both laugh as I nearly fall inside it. The inside is rotten, soft as the brown bits in an apple.

'Picked it up at a moving sale,' Mick answers. 'It'll have to go.' Then: 'Did you see that chipmunk run behind the sofa?'

'No,' I say, disappointed. 'I was looking out the window. So many trees. Seven acres. I can't believe they're all ours.'

'The pines with the spindly branches at the end, kind of Japanese looking – that's Ponderosa. The really big ones are Douglas Firs, they drop the cones with twin-pointed scales, that's how you can tell, then the others are mostly Lodgepole, that's the kind Indians used to make canoes out of, and we've also got some Tamarack, the locals call it Western Larch.'

Mick starts whistling, then asks 'Well doll, fancy a cuppa?' doing his cockney accent. I look around for a kettle and spot one, on the floor, but no stove. Following my gaze, Mick whacks me on the bum, saying, 'No good looking at the kettle, we need *water* first . . .'

'You can't keep your hands off me for a minute,' I tell him, standing on tiptoes to kiss his neck, and managing to whack him back at the same time.

Mick pretends to run away from me, pushes the door. He has scooped up Frances and a water container – a square blue plastic bottle with 5 Gallons in raised writing on the side – he must have brought *that* too, or else it was left here. I jump down off the deck of the cabin, there's a knack to this, choosing the right board to leap from, one that doesn't spring or wobble, and I trot behind him, staring at the muscles in his thighs, his hairy legs in his shorts. Amazing how quickly Mick tans.

First lesson is how to get water up from the pump. The

well, I discover, is about 200 yards from the cabin, down the drive, kicking at the pine cones, across the gravel road we just drove up, and along a path lined with brambles, a mess of pine trees. Something moves, and Frances squeaks with joy. 'Chipmunk,' Mick says again. 'There's loads of them.'

It's not what I would call a well, it's not sunken, and there's no bucket, but perhaps those are just the things in nursery rhymes, places a kitten falls into? This well is a giant stone cylinder, with a cement circle for a lid, and a rickety-handled pump. It stands in the middle of a large puddle which Mick calls a creek; the skin of the water is pitted with spidery-legged water beetles. 'Yuk!' I say, and Mick calls me a sissy.

He gives me a choice between pumping the water, or holding steady the small neck of the blue container to catch it. Since I don't know what either entails, I shrug and say, 'I'll watch Frances in case she falls in the creek . . .' which is the wrong reply. Trying to make amends I opt to steady the container at the bottom of the pipe while Mick works the arm of the pump. This, I realise from the effort he's putting in, is easier if you use two hands. The pipe is cobwebby, looks dirty to me, and the icy water splashing out of it and over my hand is the colour of urine. Frances crowds me, getting her T-shirt soaked trying to muscle in, the container is too heavy, I'm scared I'll drop it. 'Rita, keep the pipe steady,' Mick shouts, his arm pumping furiously. Frances and I are standing in a mud puddle where my aim has directed the pipe anywhere but into the container, my shoulder is aching already from the weight of it, my right hand with the water splashing over it is freezing.

'Oh, for God's sake, Rita, put some effort into it!' Mick explodes and Frances and I jump back. I notice out of the corner of my eye a tiny movement of Frances's head, not quite a duck, but a readiness to duck, and I wonder if I have the same look? We both stand still, hands by our sides as Mick steadies himself, continues pumping with one hand and with the other snatches the container from my hand. With it full to splashing he marches down the short brambly path, crosses the gravel road without looking behind him and strides up our drive. He is leaning determinedly over to one side, the weight of the water carrier is too much for him, I can see every muscle on his back straining, but this time he doesn't ask me to help. There is nothing to do but trail behind him, wiping my wet hands on the back of my thighs. Frances trots at a ferocious pace, trying to catch her father up. As she passes me she aims an idle kick in my direction and misses.

'Next time, you can fetch the water,' Mick mutters, when we reach the cabin.

'Sorry,' I say. There is a pause. I stand awkwardly for a moment, then I try running my hand just under the hem of his shorts, which makes him wriggle and set the container down, splashing brown spots on the dusty cabin floor. His expression changes and I smile back, relieved.

Mick makes the tea, carefully showing me first how to light the stove, and where he's putting the matches (out of Frances's reach). There is a strong puff of fuel, the little Colman fire is rusty and wobbly, a blue and purple tongue licks viciously at the bottom of the kettle. ('Do you recognise this stove?' Mick asks, gleefully. 'It's that one I bought off Spider for 50p, I sent it over in the Box.') I start folding up the blankets, then try stretching out on the mattress. Not bad.

'Where d'you get this?' I ask him. It's better than the bed in the squat back home, an ancient, pancake-flat futon. It's positively luxurious, compared to that.

'Picked it up at Mo and Pete's. Said we could have it. Brought it out here the first time. Good, eh?'

Mo and Pete are Mick's in-laws. That is, the parents of Carole, his brother Jon's wife, does that make them in-laws? I'm not too sure of these rules, not being married we don't have any in-laws, it's the sort of thing I've avoided, like office parties and christenings. Having Frances has pushed me into some of it, I can cope with children's birthday parties now, but I dread her going to school. Parents' Day, picking her up from school, the normal things, mixing with other people, getting up at a certain time, even setting an alarm clock. So much that I've managed to avoid so far.

We've no idea what the time is, but despite her nap Frances is obviously tired; rubbing her eyes and cranky. It's a good job we ate at the café, that nobody's hungry, because there's nothing, and I can't imagine how far the nearest shop might be. I can't imagine anything out here; cooking, shopping, bathing ... even the loo, a wooden out-house with no door and a plastic toilet seat, placed over the hole in a box of plyboard, makes no sense to me; being on a slight hill behind the cabin, won't all that crap flow down, towards the cabin? Mick says just piss anywhere, what does it matter, this is our land, after all, and Frances at least takes him at his word, delighted to have her nappy off.

After drinking our tea we stand in the doorway, and shrug at the view. 'Nine o'clock?' Mick tries. It's still light, but a dull grey light, sunless, trees dipping into a small valley at our right, green barriers to light, to the rest of the world. I can hear a dog, faraway, it must belong to our neighbour, Mick says we have one. And tiny, sharp little cries, musical – are they crickets or cicadas? They sound like a film soundtrack.

Mick sets up the travel cot Carole has given us, and heaves the other sofa from the truck, with some clumsy help from me. With Frances settled, in her pyjamas, two sweaters and two pairs of socks, we make up our bed for the night on the mattress, Mick's old duvet from the squat, no pillows or sheets, two blankets thrown on top. I keep my clothes on, rough wool under my chin, I'm *freezing*. Mick snuggles up to me, his chest to my back, puts his hands under my layers of sweaters. Before he gets far I swat at his hands. They feel like spiders creeping under my clothes. I grab them and hold tight.

'I'm too cold, Mick. I don't want to get this lot off. It was so hot in the daytime. Is it always like this at night?'

'Yeah. That's this area for you. Don't worry, it'll be better when the glass is in, and I'll make a stove out of an oil barrel. I've got a book on it.'

I release my hold on his hands and he continues creeping his fingers up inside the tight jumper, breathing snuffily in my ear.

'Just pull your leggings down. Leave the jumpers on if you're cold,' he whispers.

Just before he falls asleep, I say, 'Mick, will you put the glass in tomorrow? I hate those open windows. Are there wild animals out here? What if a bear came along, or . . .'

No reply. He's rolled over, his body is heavy and still.

'Mick . . .' I whisper. The cabin is dark when we close the front door, a potent, unusual dark, like being in a cave, but of course we have to close the door. I change my mind, I don't want to say it, there's too much silence here, it's palpable, like another body breathing in the room.

'It will be all right, won't it?' I mumble.

'What?' His voice comes from a long way off, the edge of sleep. The bed smells of cigarettes, cold, damp, of our camping trip to Scotland.

'You did promise, Mick. You are going to be, you know, *calm*, you do feel happy, don't you and we are going to get on . . .'

His snores tell me he's already asleep. I don't know myself what I was going to say. I lie for a long time with the cold outdoor taste in my mouth, listening to every twig creak, every blade of grass move; my woolly, swaddled chest pressed up hard against Mick's naked, hot back. He never seems to feel the cold the way I do.

## 4

A thud on the cabin roof jolts me awake. I lie with my eyes wide open – the darkness doesn't alter – wondering what it could be. I'm just about to shake Mick awake, when I realise. A pine cone dropping from a tree. I heard the same thing in the afternoon, too, but then the sound had seemed quieter.

My heart is beating quickly and although I close my eyes again and snuggle up against Mick's back, it doesn't calm down. I feel as if I've drunk ten cups of coffee, my thoughts buzzing, pictures, memories, bad dreams.

The night I met Mick was the night I was attacked. Of course the two events weren't connected but one never pops into my head without the other. It's about eight or eight-thirty, I'm on my way to the pub, my guitar with me, swinging against my legs. It's dark, that London dreary dark, and it's drizzling a bit, Richmond Road is lined with wet, shining cars, the street-lights on, making each car the same sour yellow colour; I'm hurrying – I'm usually late for gigs – and I hear steps running behind me.

I think it's someone I know. Someone catching up with me, to tell me something. I've lived in Dalston for a long time, I don't worry that much, I walk briskly, I take the bus where possible, I'm wearing my monkey boots. I pause.

And the shock. Feeling the arms go round my neck and

the weight of someone suddenly behind me, and my knees folding, and the crack and pain as they hit the pavement. And tumbling, ungainly, letting go of the guitar case and hearing it skid across the ground – feeling the weight now on my shoulders and back, my nose near the pavement, and without my glasses I can only see a grey, wet blur. And then the crunching pain in my arm, awkwardly bent beneath me, as someone falls on it – or maybe it's me, my own weight nearly breaking the elbow, and the pain in my chest and throat. I can't breathe, a gasping feeling that is maybe caused by his arms around my neck, or maybe not that, not caused by anyone, only fear.

'What the fuck – ing – hell?' I'm amazed to find I can shout, jump up, he's no longer on top of me. I'm screaming in a second, staring straight at him, he is up and standing too.

'What the fuck do you think you're doing? You bastard!' My voice so much louder than I expect, my rage a complete surprise to me, so instant, my heart leaping and thumping with a violence fit to break my ribcage. Reaching for the guitar case, and noticing that it is now streaked with wet and dirt, and him still standing there, staring at me, paralysed, and I see that he is very young, he's wearing a woolly hat, and a blue sweater, although he is tall, he is very young, sixteen or eighteen; younger than me.

He makes a move, a small jerky move with his hand towards me. Something flashes, a knife? But it could be a bracelet at his wrist, a ring, nothing really, a trick of the light, without my glasses how can I tell?

'Fuck off, you stupid git!' I yell, feeling my face pulling into shapes, a face I haven't felt since childhood – pure, vicious, ugly. An explosion inside me. I shake from head to toe, my body bursts sweat from every pore. I'm striding away from him as fast as possible, swinging the guitar again. I'm bending to brush my stinging knee with one hand, brushing the grit from the soft, bloodied hole in my tights, not looking over my shoulder, daring to turn my back to him although it makes the hairs on the nape of my neck prickle and then hearing his steps, him running in the other direction, away from me. His trainers on a wet pavement, fading.

Why? Why me? What was he going to do?

By the time I get to the pub I'm more worried about the amp and the pick-up and my tights being laddered (I take them off in the pub toilet, risking raw white legs). Standing in that tiny little room, leaning over the sink to check myself in the mirror (unless my nose is practically on the glass I can't see a thing) five minutes before I'm due to go on and I suddenly retch, bringing up my tea in the poxy little sink. Three-bean salad mingles with smears of liquid soap.

Maybe it's pre-gig nerves. That's normal enough. I've only been singing in pubs for about a year, trying to supplement the dole and make enough money for my training. I'm in my first year of training to be a psychotherapist. A day job's no good because it inteferes with the lectures and study and the therapy I have to undergo as part of the course; a part-time job won't do because the DSS takes everything I earn. Pubs pay cash.

Where's Mick while I'm singing? I don't know. I'm fixing my gaze somewhere on the floor two yards away from me. Sometimes I close my eyes. I'm self-conscious about having bare legs, with a skirt this short I need opaque tights – the black cotton sort that don't show anything – because I'm trying to rest the guitar on my bent knee. I sing 'Too Tired' and 'I Gotta Leave This Neighborhood/Nobody Loves Me But My Mother', changing all the 'women' to 'boys'. The line about the 'six-foot woman with a knife in her hand coming after me' gets a weak laugh from a woman at the bar.

I finish – put the guitar down, mutter 'thank you' to no one in particular – two people clap and the landlord puts the juke-box back on. Then I'm standing at the bar, right up close to Mick, I see him for the first time; I'm staring at his profile, the silver stud in his nose, the short blond hair, the collar up on his leather jacket. I'm wondering what to order – the pub is the real ale sort, and I don't know the names of the beers.

He says, 'Shouldn't leave your guitar there. Someone might nick it.'

I grunt something. I'm not receptive to being chatted up after a gig, men always want to tell me what a great guitar player they are, or that a woman Blues guitarist just doesn't work. Mick doesn't say any of that. He buys me a half of bitter. He has an American twang to his voice and I ask him about that, find out that he grew up in the States, mostly Wisconsin, but his Dad was English, from Nottingham. He left the States six years ago, chasing an English girlfriend, but that fell through. He wants to go back sometime.

He takes the jacket off and buys us more drinks. He smokes roll-ups, Golden Virginia tobacco, green Rizla papers, expertly licked. His arms are like men's arms in cartoons. Curved. Like Pop-Eye arms.

'You should have a pipe, and some spinach,' I say. I splurt into giggles. We talk more. He buys us more drinks.

Later, we stumble to his squat two streets from the pub, a huge Edwardian house, with three storeys, tatty pieces of carpet everywhere, original fire-place, the futon on the floor. Without his Clash T-shirt I see that he has fine blond hair all over his chest, and a tattoo which he tries to cover up, laughing, a tattoo which says something like Cherie-Rose, and is faded, a weird kind of green. 'An ex. Nothing for you to worry about. I was only fifteen . . . my Mum nearly killed me when I had that done,' he says. His profile again, this time silhouetted in the semi-dark in his bedroom. I tell him he looks like Mr Punch from Punch and Judy. 'In other words, you've got a big nose.' But having grown up in the States he doesn't know who Mr Punch is.

I go through my entire routine; venture everything from a

clumsy strip, flicking my knickers up in the air off my big toe and attempting to catch them (I fall over) to a badly executed sixty-nine (I choke, misjudge and nearly throw up again).

Mick pats my backside gently and whispers in my ear, 'Anyone ever tell you you're a crap singer?' I collapse onto the futon and we both laugh for a long time.

When I tell Mick about the attack he says: 'Strikes me that someone like you can look after herself.' I love that. That pleases me. I kiss him for that; he pulls me down into his face, one hand on the back of my head, his other on the back of my thighs.

I shift position in bed, place my face against the skin of Mick's back and kiss it as lightly as I can, making sure I don't wake him. My heartbeat won't slow to normal, I can still feel it pattering away, like footsteps. Like feet on an empty street, running. Did anything terrible really happen, did something terrible nearly happen? My mouth is dry. I didn't try to run, I didn't freeze, I stood my ground. I even fought back. That surprises me, even now. I suppose no one knows how they'll respond to danger until they find themselves in it. We think we know, but we might be wrong. But the troubling bit is something else; it's deciding. It's not knowing. Which part of me is exaggerating, which to be trusted? The part that pictures the knife, dirty-metal and smeared with blood, or the part that thinks that's silly and hysterical, part of the TV world, a fantasy?

It's morning, I'm lying stiff as a peg doll, Frances's wailing dragging me from a restless sleep full of small rustlings; tiny noises, pricking me into wakefulness. Opening my eyes I catch sight of a chipmunk for the first time as it scurries along the floor beside the bed, carrying a piece of orange peel. It's much smaller than I imagined – not much bigger than a mouse – and, though I hated the mice we once had in the squat, this cute little thing with the black stripe along its orange side and the beady black eye and fluffy tail is fine, much nicer. I have no urge to scream.

Mick is still sleeping, amazingly, given the racket Frances is making. As I get out of bed, my toe touches my glasses in their case on the floor but I don't stop to put them on, I pick up a coiled, sprung child from her travel cot and try to unwind her. Her wails continue as I carry her to what could laughably be described as the window, being in fact, a large square gap through which light and heat is pouring in.

- 'Look at the trees, Frances. Look at the lovely trees out there. That's a *big* pine tree and that's a – um . . .'

Frances shows no interest at all but twists pitifully in my arms until I let her down. There she cries even more, looking around herself in furious horror, her pyjamas stuck to her. She's always soaking in the mornings, drinks too much juice before going to sleep. Her face has a few pink patches, she might have been bitten by mosquitoes, I forgot to plaster her in bug repellent before I put her to bed. Guilt, guilt. Or maybe she was frightened, maybe she's missing her Auntie Nicola or reacting to the journey . . . I find myself, as usual, searching for explanations, adult ones that I can deal with. Heart-felt, pure baby sounds are the worst in the world.

'For Christ's sake, Frances,' Mick mutters, stuffing his head under the duvet.

I struggle with the cabin door, with Frances in my arms. I want to take her outside, surely the sight of all that land, that huge play area will calm her, compensate for the loss of her auntie, her toys, her little world of cot mobiles and board books. 'It'll be all right,' I whisper, into her soft scented cheek but she resists any kind of comforting, this child, her screams in my ear rattle my head like a blow. I feel as if she hates me.

The wooden door suddenly gives, and we almost fall outwards. Our loud exit startles something that was outside, on the deck, I hear a flap and then I see it: a huge blue bird.

The colour is stunning, the blue of a TV screen, electric blue, that kind of blue is a real colour then, not what I thought, something technological.

Frances is so astonished she closes her mouth for a moment, flings a little fat arm towards it. The bird, black crested, crow-sized, heads for the trees, a sharp screech uttering its surprise, or dismay, at finding us there.

# 5

I find some plastic sandals for Frances and plant her on the deck. With her nappy off, some pieces of orange to munch on, and the ants running over the greying wooden boards of the deck to entertain her, she quietens down. Best not to wake Mick. I take off the clothes I slept in and find some shorts and a black cotton vest from my rucksack, find my glasses, tie my hair back with an elastic band, then sit down beside her, on the warm wood. Some of the boards are broken, rusty nails protrude from others; long grasses sprout between them.

I put my glasses on, gaze out, up to spindly branches which form the tops of the tallest trees, where the blue bird disappeared. It's hard to believe we're half way up a mountain – where's the view? I suppose it's because we're not on the face of the mountain and of course, the trees make you feel enclosed. Some pines are tall and healthy, a couple are twig-like, grey and dried. Apart from that, I can't see how Mick can spot all those differences between them, surely they're all the same; varying heights and trunk-widths maybe, but aren't they just pine trees?

'What do you think, hmm Frances? Here we are. What do you make of it?'

She puts a huge piece of orange in her mouth, lets the juices squirt out. Carries on poking the ants with a stick. I tip my head back, push my glasses onto my nose with one finger.

What do *I* make of it? It must be eighty degrees already. The
sky is a clean sheet of blue, the sun is balanced on the highest
branch of all, so that direction must be the East, or is that the
West, I can't remember where the sun rises? What a basic
question, I couldn't possibly ask Mick, he'd never believe I
didn't know. I can smell wood, cedar wood and burnt wood
and bark, and pine, I can definitely smell that although it's
nothing like air freshener or toilet cleaner. I can hear birds,
birds everywhere, really noisy birds, chirping and burbling
in a way that I haven't heard for years. Lying on the school
playing fields chewing a piece of grass was the last time I
heard birds like these. And a truck. An engine. I can hear
a truck.

'Mick! Someone's coming, a truck's coming up the road!'

I open the door to the cabin wide, let the light stream onto
the mattress, and Mick emerges from under the duvet and
the blankets, squinting.

'Well don't panic, Rita. They might just be going up the
road to the spring. Or to the lake. There's a lake at the top
of the mountain. Top Lake.'

'No, no it's coming through the trees at the bottom of our
drive. A green truck, I mean, a what's-it-called – a pick-up.
I can see it!'

Slowly, he peels the duvet off. Pauses to grin, and say, 'Look
what I've got for you,' then readjusts himself, tucking his offer
into his underpants. He puts some shorts and a T-shirt on. By
which time, the pick-up has stopped right outside the deck.
The engine dies. A door slams.

'Hi there! Mick, you home?'

'It's Jim,' Mick whispers, standing behind me, prodding me
out towards the door. 'Our neighbour, the one I met when I
came up here to buy it. Don't worry, he's fine.'

So we both go out onto the deck, where this bearded,
hairy creature in faded jeans, bare feet and a checked shirt
is standing. The sun dips in behind a tiny cloud. Frances stops

poking the ants and stands up for a moment, watching. I'm reminded absurdly of *Gunfight at the OK Corral*. My eyes rest on his belt, then on his hands. In one of them he carries a six-pack of beer.

Mick says, 'Hi, Jim, hello – this is the wife, Rita.' I want to say 'He's joking – we're not married,' but decide it would sound funny, so I smile and shake the hand that Jim is offering, trying not to stare. His hand is enormous; my rings crush into me under his rigorous shake and his palm feels smooth, hardened.

'Good to meet you Rita. And who's the little guy?'

'That's Frances. She's a girl.'

Of course she's a girl, she's practically naked. Mick and Jim laugh, Mick says, 'Rita can't get used to the way Americans use "guy" for everything . . .'

This breaks the ice, at least. Mick pulls up two up-ended log-ends, sits on one, offers Jim the other. I sit on the floor of the deck.

'So, you're English, Rita? Not half and half like Mick?'

'Yes. We are. English. Me and the baby, I mean. I met Mick in London.'

Jim studies me. Aside from the ZZ-Top image, which I've never seen before outside of a music video, he has a nice face. Deepset brown eyes and a sharp mouth, almost obscured behind a long dark beard, and hair with a couple of streaks of grey, matting into the beard, so that it's impossible to work out where the hair stops and the beard begins. Frances has a troll with hair like that.

'You guys better watch the sun. Your skin's pretty fair,' Jim says. My hand automatically goes up to my hair, which feels scratty and tangled. I've just got out of bed, I suddenly think, I must look awful.

Mick passes Jim a yellow packet of Top tobacco and Jim carefully licks a cigarette paper, then feels in the back pocket of his jeans for something.

'I brought you guys a present. A bit of home-grown skunk weed.'

The plastic bag of grass he passes Mick is enormous. They both laugh. Jim offers Mick a can of beer, Milwaukee, which he takes, and then me.

'What time is it?' I ask. Beer for breakfast?

'Oh hell. You're on Mount Coyote time now. Who cares?'

The two of them swig beer and after a pause I open my can. Cold light liquid pours down my throat.

'Me, me!' says Frances, putting her hot cheek up to the can, trying to poke her nose down the hole.

'We didn't bring much food,' says Mick. 'First thing we've got to do is go for supplies, also buy a cool box, and today I need to put the windows in – we only arrived last night. We haven't even unpacked yet.'

'Yeah – I heard you. Heard your truck, and Nancy heard the kid crying this morning . . .'

I'm surprised to discover they can hear us from wherever it is they live. Must be their dogs I heard last night. Mount Coyote is a mystery to me, there could be houses everywhere but the feeling of isolation would be the same. It's the lack of telegraph wires, noises, aeroplanes, and the screen of trees. You can't even see the road from the cabin.

'What happened to your truck?' I ask, noticing that his pick-up, parked next to ours, has a smashed windscreen, spider webs spinning out from a first-sized crack.

Jim grins at Mick as if he has already told him the story. He takes a swig of beer. I think for an instant that he's ignoring my question, then after another mouthful of beer, he says: 'Long story. Long story, man.' Another pause. He draws on the spliff he's made, passes it to Mick, starts again. 'I'm not getting down, you understand? That fucking Smokey, I love him like a brother.'

He seems to be talking to Mick, not me. But I'm wondering why Mick would know so much about it, when after all, as far as I can make out, Mick only met Jim once before, the first time he came up here, to buy the land.

Jim finishes his can of beer, opens another one. Although Mick's is half-full he offers him another, an automatic gesture. I'm puzzling over the phrase 'not getting down', which I don't understand.

'Smokey's OK, he's OK, I don't want to – poison you to him,' Jim says. 'But – hey there's one thing I can't stand and that's a guy beating up on his old lady. I'm a sexist pig. Yeah, I admit that. But when I drive to Smokey's place, late at night, maybe to have a few beers or yeah, something like that, and I see him beating up on his old lady – well, maybe I'm wrong you know? I should keep the fuck out of things. My nose out of other people's business. That's what Nancy says. We had this problem before. I'm a peaceful guy. All this peace and love shit, that's me. And I love that guy like a brother. Well, Smokey's old lady's only small. Elly. She's one hundred pounds, tops. She works at the gas station in Goldtown. So, all I do, I just tried to separate them. I tell him, Hey Smokey, take it easy. She's screamin' an' all that shit. I just tried to get between Smokey and her and he knocked out two of my teeth.'

He opens his mouth to show me. Then grins, wearily.

'Jeez, that guy's like a brother to me. He knocks out two of my teeth, and then he takes a rock to my truck. I say Smokey, take it easy, hey! But then I decide, Jesus, it's not worth it. I'll get the fuck outa here. Two missing teeth and one cracked window. End of story.'

'Couldn't you call the police? Did you go to the police, about your truck, I mean?' I ask.

'What, you see any payphones up here on the mountain?' Jim laughs. I feel silly. Of course there aren't any payphones, no one has a phone, so what do they do in an emergency?

'Mostly we sort it out ourselves. If there's a fire, we radio. Channel six. You have a CB?'

'Not yet,' Mick replies. 'I'm working on it.'

'Use ours,' Jim offers. 'No problem. We're your nearest neighbour. Just run down to our place.'

'What if there was an accident? A murder?' I persist. 'I mean, sometimes people on Mount Coyote must have occasion to need the police . . .'

'Last time I saw a police car up here was 1989. Chasing some kids in a stolen Pontiac Firebird. They don't want to wreck their police vehicles' (he draws these words out – poeleece veehickles) 'if they can help it, you understand. No, like I say, we mostly like to sort out our own problems. Bruce still has a bullet hole in his pants from messing with Fisher's old lady. That's justice Mount Coyote style.'

The pride in his voice is unmistakable. I feel like I'm back in the squat, listening to Mick and Spider talking about evictions and signing-on scams. I can share it up to a point. But when they talk about the pigs, I feel differently. I might need the 'pigs' one day. In fact I never use the word, I don't know many women who do.

'Was this Smokey pissed?' I ask, to keep the conversation going.

'Pissed – sure, he wanted to knock my teeth out, sure he was pissed with me . . .'

Mick intervenes, a cultural misunderstanding, he's spotted it immediately.

'No, Jim, Rita means drunk, you know. In England pissed means drunk.'

Jim nods, raising an eyebrow. 'Oh yeah, sure he was drunk. We're always drunk. We're a bunch of alcoholics up here, you know that?'

He's glamorising the mountain again. It's lawlessness, it's difference. I don't know why it's irritating me so much.

'Doesn't mean he can beat up on his old lady,' Jim pronounces, firmly.

'No, of course not.' I dart a glance at Mick. His head is

down, concentrating on rolling another spliff, the silver stud in his nose catches the sun and glitters for a moment. He looks up, his voice is neutral.

'Jim. I want to ask you a question. Do you know anyone round here who has found any gold on their property?'

# 6

Jim stands up. I think that he is ignoring a question again, but then it occurs to me that maybe it's just his habit. He takes a very long time to answer.

'Gold,' he says, running one hand through his matted hair, stretching his back a little in the sun.

He steps down from the deck, walks a few paces away from the cabin, turns his back and unzips the fly on his jeans.

'Yeah, sure there might be some gold. The biggest gold mine in the USA is just thirty miles from here, at Republic. Some. Not much I guess. But that gold's not yours. No sirree fucking bob. You can't keep it.'

Frances says 'wee' and makes swishing noises. I don't know where to look, I find it incredible that someone I've just met would take a leak while still talking to me, so I sip my beer, stare into my can. Mick says, 'What d'you mean, it's not ours?'

Jim turns around, tucking the checked shirt into his jeans, adjusting his belt.

'You signed some kind of deed when you bought this property, yeah?' Mick nods. 'Well, that deed says any oil or mineral rights belong to the Lot Range, that's the Department you bought the land from. They keep any gold you find. Or any oil, or anything else for that fuckin' matter.'

Mick is bending down to do his trainers up, he seems unconcerned but when he looks up he says, 'You know this land don't you? I mean, before I bought it didn't you say you used to walk through it on your way over to Smokey's place?'

'Sure.'

'Would you do me a favour . . . come and look at this rocky bit, tell me how likely a spot you think it would be for blasting—'

'Mick, you're joking aren't you? What on earth would you "blast" it with? We haven't even got any knives and forks yet, let alone a few handy sticks of dynamite . . .'

They both laugh, but they're stepping down from the deck, Mick in front, Jim, barefoot has to take it more slowly, his feet crunching the hard grass, avoiding pine cones. Mick wants to walk west of the cabin, it's downhill, and there's a smallish clearing where trees become sparse, but it's through tangled shrubs, mini pine trees and the dying arnica flowers, a jumble of things. It's hard to make out where one plant ends and another begins. Jim seems doubtful.

'Man, I need shoes,' he mutters, slowing down.

I have Frances in my arms and she makes a dive for something at her level, a pale pink flower, opened, about the size of her hand, on top of a bush.

'Looks like a kind of wild rose. A dog rose?' I suggest.

'That's Nootka rose,' says Jim. 'You know rose-hips? Nancy makes some kinda jelly from them.'

Frances crushes the flower in her fist, lets the crumbled petals scatter. I look around for another but they're all tucked away, and the bush looks thorny.

Jim calls, 'Hey, Mick, I can't walk on your place today. I need shoes,' coming to a halt and swaying slightly, arm dangling by his side, holding the beer can. He lets some trickle out and I realise how stoned he must be, and how giddy I am, drinking beer on an empty stomach.

Mick stops, his back to us. He's pointing.

'It's that rocky bit, just there. The trees thin out and there are a couple of boulders, stuck together. It looks like someone tried to dig a well behind it, but gave up. I was thinking, I must put a plank or something over it, to make it safe for Frances. If they were looking for water, and found it too hard to dig, maybe no one's ever dug for gold there either?'

'Maybe,' Jim says, but to me he doesn't sound convinced. He's heading back towards the cabin, weaving between tree-stumps and bushes and I follow, with Frances squealing to be put down. A blue bird, the kind with the black crest that we saw this morning, skirts over the treetops, crawing noisily.

'What's that bird? Its colour is amazing . . .' I ask the back of Jim's head.

'Blue jay. Nancy calls them camp robbers, but I think the real name's something like Stellar's Jay. I don't rightly know, you know, names in books. I just know what the fuck we call stuff and I call that a blue jay.'

At the cabin he gets in his pick-up, sits in the driver's seat behind his cracked windscreen rolling another spliff, before starting the engine. Mick comes striding back, carrying a tyre that he's picked up and dumping it with the other junk at the front of the cabin.

Jim sticks his head out of the window. 'I forgot. I'm supposed to invite you guys over sometime. The old lady said to ask you. Drop by, anytime, and meet the kids. She says, Welcome to Mount Coyote.'

'You're not serious about looking for gold, Mick, are you?'

We're in the truck. The plastic is so hot my bare thighs are sticking to it and Frances shrieked while I strapped her into the baby-seat, when I accidentally touched her with the hot metal clasp. I wedge a tea-towel between her stomach and the metal. There would be no point pulling her T-shirt down, given that it always rides up over her round belly.

Mick pushes the gear-stick into drive, turns left at the end of our driveway. In the middle of the gravel road – wide enough only for one pick-up – he stops, reaches for his Top tobacco balanced between the dashboard and the windscreen.

'Yeah, I'm serious. Why not? There might be something. I mean, this is the route. During the gold rush in the 1890s people would have come up this way to Alaska from Seattle. The biggest find of all, apart from California was the Yukon. Dawson City. Well, maybe most people heading for the Yukon would have come via the coast, but some must have gone overland. Via Okanogan . . . Why d'you think it's called Goldtown if there's no gold?'

'But this is 1991! All the gold would have been found by now, surely . . .'

'Not necessarily. I mean, who owned our property before the Lot Developers? Indians! Jim says Mount Coyote's only been lived on by whites in the last fifty years or so, since the last forest fire. And since the gold rush was mostly about getting to Dawson and the Yukon, maybe plenty of smaller places got missed out on the way.'

He reaches in the pocket of his shorts for the huge plastic bag of skunk weed that Jim gave him, tips a little into the cigarette paper, is just about to lick it and roll it when Frances makes a lunge, grabs at the paper in his hand and knocks the lot onto his knee.

'Oh fucking hell!' Mick spits out. He brushes the tobacco, paper and grass from his knee. 'Fucking child,' he says under his breath.

'For God's sake, Mick, she didn't mean to do it. It was an accident . . .'

Mick puts the truck into drive again, stares straight ahead. We drive in silence for a while, the only vehicle on the road, winding through trees, climbing. Every so often a burst of tall crimson flowers appear at the side of the gravel road, then occasionally a tall enormous thistle, red brush on top. Instead of going down the mountain towards Sinkalip, we're driving up towards Top Lake, intending to go down the other side of the mountain into Goldtown to do some shopping. Mick says it will have bigger stores, being almost in Canada, the first stop for tourists entering the USA. 'Or the last for those going to Canada,' I say, preferring to think of it that way, as a town which is almost Canada, rather than a town which is freshly America. I'm beginning to have a better sense of our location, Mount Coyote is between these two towns, about eight miles from each. Goldtown is two miles off the border of British Columbia.

Mick looks tired. He rubs his forehead with a sweaty palm and leaves his blond fringe sticking up, slightly damp, as if he'd hair-gelled it. I realise that he is annoyed at driving so much; a whole day driving yesterday and now this. He successfully rolls another smoke, driving with one hand on the wheel, draws on it, starts talking again.

'What's your problem with me asking Jim about gold?'

'I just think it's, well – silly. It seems foolish and – unlikely – and I mean, wouldn't you need special equipment and stuff.'

'I'm not talking about huge amounts, Rita. A small amount would be fine. I could rig up a drill easy enough, maybe use an old car engine. I'm gonna ask Jim and this guy Buster that he mentioned, he's done some panning—'

'But I thought we were here to get away from all of that?'

'What do you mean?'

'Well, you know, to live – like, not like we lived in London. Simply.'

'Well fucking hell, Rita, how do you think we *are* going to live, out here, with no fucking money?'

'But we've got some money, we've got my savings—'

'They won't last long!'

'I thought you were going to work in the orchards or in Sinkalip or something?'

'Yeah, sure you thought *I* was going to do all the work—'

'I didn't! I mean, Nicola's still signing on for me in London and she said she'd send some dole over, so we can have that for the next few weeks until she gets scared, and we won't need so many things out here and—'

'Oh yeah, we won't need so many things – only a fucking generator and a cool box and some new roofing and God, you're fucking stupid sometimes.'

'Don't call me stupid! And stop fucking swearing so much, in front of Frances!'

I make an angry gesture with my hand, a dismissive wipe, as if to stifle the swearing and that's too much for Mick. He curses again, screeches to a halt, nearly banging both our heads on the windscreen and starts bellowing.

'Get out then, bitch. If you don't like my swearing, get out and fucking walk!'

'Oh I will, don't worry!' I shout, my voice a shriek, little and sharp beneath Mick's enormous boom. My hand is on the inside handle, opening the door. Mick slams it shut again, leaning over Frances, who is crying at all the noise; Mick shouting, the door slamming. Mick's hand is over my hand, grappling with me over the door. He suddenly changes tack, puts the truck in drive and the door flaps open with me nearly falling out.

'You're such a bastard,' I say, using all my weight to pull the door closed. He stops again. Switches the engine off. Silence.

'What did you say, Rita?'

Silence again. He gets out and walks round to my side and in the windscreen I see the set of his face in profile, grim, the big nose, the silver pin.

'Rita. I asked you a question. What did you call me?'

I say nothing, sit with my heart thumping, biting the skin on the side of my nails.

'Come on. Out,' he says. He opens the door for me. I step out.

I stand as defiantly as I dare, hands on hips, the thumping in my chest louder and louder.

He puts his face up very close to mine, the pupils wide, black obscuring the blue.

'Rita. Why – don't – you – drive – if – you – are – so – fucking – cle-ver.'

Between each word he prods me with his finger, pushing me against the warm metal door of the car. Each prod leaves a thudding sting in the bony part of my chest. I stare down at his finger.

'Mick, I – let's stop now, it's nothing – I'm sorry – you're tired and we're both hungry and exhausted and I don't know why we're having this argument—'

He makes a sudden movement, a movement so fast that my breath catches, but then he seems to change his mind and instead he yells, a weird noise between a yelp and a roar, and thumps the bonnet of the truck with his fist. Frances answers with a frightened shriek.

'Get in the car,' he says, and starts the engine.

## 7

Frances is napping, strapped in her baby-seat in the truck with her head lolling and the tea-towel scrunched up to her chin. It must be after midday, the sun was overhead but now it's lower, at the same level as the roof of the cabin. The light is creamy, making long shadows.

We're lying on a scratchy rug, sludge-coloured, on the ground near the truck. I'm in shorts and my bra, Mick in his shorts. The sun makes the hairs on his chest lighter than ever. He leans on his side on one elbow, looking at me and not speaking. I'm on my stomach trying to read but because my face is sweating my glasses keep slipping down and the page is smeared the letters dancing.

'You have such a beautiful ass,' he says, his American copshow accent.

I don't say anything, swat at a buzzing fly. Out of the corner of my eye I notice the flicker in the shrubs of a chipmunk, scurrying to the end of one fine long twig, and then balancing, weighting the twig to a curve, nose twitching, hands up to its face.

Mick puts his hand on my shorts. He rests it there, I feel the palm through thin checked cotton and the muscles in my buttocks tense, then relax. I'm reading the *Book of Western Forests*, looking up the deer we saw on the way back from

Goldtown. It was a White-tail, I saw the tail flagging as it ran into the trees, away from us.

I hear Mick draw on his smoke. He breathes out.

'Beautiful everything,' he says softly.

He moves his hand from my bottom to my neck, waits to see if I'll shake it off. I don't. He gathers up my hair, holds it into a ponytail and my neck feels cool and relieved. I make a tiny sigh. He kisses my neck and the blood gathers there.

'Lovely Rita, Meter-maid,' he sings to me. I'm still trying to read – 'When nervous, White-tails snort through their noses and stamp their hooves . . .' I feel sweat trickle down my armpit.

Mick carries on kissing my neck, lets the hair fall back down on it, begins stroking my breast, tracing the lace edge of the bra – lightly, as if he doesn't mean it, as if it's incidental and his mind is elsewhere, he could lift his hand off anytime but he couldn't, I know he couldn't. My breath comes tightly.

He undoes the catch on the bra. It falls forward onto the page, a black shadow across it. I help him by slipping my arms out of the straps, taking my glasses off and lying them beside me.

'Rita. I'm sorry.'

'It's OK.'

'You know I'm sorry . . .'

'Yes.'

'I'm sick of driving, you know. All that driving I did in London, I was so pissed off by the end . . . I'll – uh – settle in.' He puts his mouth to my breast, then my cheek, my ear. 'Rita. I love you.'

'Sometimes I think you hate me.'

'Ri-ta!'

I flap at a mosquito about to land on my shoulder and then I close my eyes. I relax down on my stomach, head down on my elbows, squashing my chest into the rough rug. Heat flows up from my toes to my forehead. I smell my own sweat strongly, and warm rubber.

'Oh – you . . .' Mick says.

Frances is still sleeping. I've been up to check her once, put a blanket over the windscreen to keep the sun from overheating her, plastered her with bug repellent, without rubbing it in so as not to wake her. On the way back to Mick on the rug I pick up two bottles of Koala Raspberry soda from the brand new cool box.

He's pulling his shorts back on. I hand him the soda. Sitting down beside him I say: 'Why are you so angry all the time? I wish I knew.'

'Well you're the therapist. You tell me.'

'I'm not a therapist, am I? I only completed the one year. Ha! Maybe I'd have found out in year two.'

'Anyhow, you're bad-tempered too, Mizz Rita Prissy-arse.'

'I know I am, I know. But. Sometimes – you really scare me.'

'Oh Rita.' He leans forward, kisses my shoulder, uncaps the soda I've been struggling with and hands it to me. He sips from his bottle.

'You know I'd never hurt you,' he says.

'Do I? I really want to – I really think that – things could be different out here, without all the stress you know? I mean, I know you hated driving a bus in London and sitting in shitty traffic all day, but you've had six weeks' break from that, I thought you'd be feeling better by now.'

'I'd feel better if you could drive. I keep saying I'll teach you.'

'Oh Mick, I've told you. I want proper lessons. You – we'll only end up arguing if you try and teach me to drive.'

'Hmm.' He rolls himself a cigarette. Stares at a chipmunk carrying an outsized Naccho chip from the deck to the bushes.

Smacks a mosquito on his thigh with one hand. A tiny black and red splat.

I rub at the splat with my forefinger. 'Yuk. Look how much blood a tiny little mosquito has in it.'

He laughs. 'That's my blood, you twit, not the mosquito's.'

I pull a face. 'Uuugh, how revolting.' I start cleaning my glasses, rubbing them against my shorts. A raven flies over, screeching, and a tiny brown bird creeps along the tyre Mick dropped on our junk pile. I swig from the bottle, wipe my mouth on my forearm. 'We own this. We could never own anything in England. Isn't that the point? I – I want it to be different out here and I'm just hoping that it's true, and I haven't made a big mistake.'

'Rita, for God's sake.' He draws on the cigarette, his eyes squinting against the smoke. 'Sometimes I'm scared of you too, you know.'

'But what could I possibly do to you?'

'Plenty.'

'Mick, you must weigh four stone more than me!'

'You could hurt me plenty.'

'We're not talking about the same thing. I give up.'

I put my glasses on and turn back to the book, flicking to the pages about birds. Stellar's Jay, I read. Mountain Quail. Common Raven. The tiny speckled brown bird on the tyre has a fat belly, and a long sharp beak. Probably a Brown Creeper. Mick lies on his back, smoking, while I leaf through the pages, sipping the pale pink liquid from the bottle. I look up the pointy stalks of crimson flowers we saw by the roadside; probably fireweed, which grows after a forest fire. All of these things, the birds, the flowers, completely ordinary. I remember once going on a school trip to Rainham Marshes, it was just before my Dad left so I must have been about six. Saying to Mr Johnston in that perky little grown-up way that I had back then, a tone reserved for teachers and my father; an attempt to impress upon both what a keen, interested child I was: 'Sir, what's that beautiful bird, the shiny black one with the yellow beak?'

He stopped in his tracks, frowned down at me, the clipboard poised in mid-air.

'Rita Barnes, haven't you ever looked in your back garden? That's a blackbird, quite common I can assure you, even in London . . .'

I faltered, but only for an instant, then recovered. 'I haven't got a back garden, sir, but I have got a balcony. We're on the sixth floor, sir. Not many birds come up there cos there's no grass. Once my brothers caught a pigeon that was crapping on my Mum's geraniums. When I wanted to keep it, she said it was a Common Pest, and pigeons carry more diseases than rats.'

Mr Johnston stared at me oddly, looking as if he was trying to decide something. Then 'Quite right too,' he said, and told me to jot down the blackbird and anything else I saw in my work-book. My Mum kept that work-book for years; careful pencil drawings and neatly printed notes. Sparow. Pidgin – a Comon Pest. Thrush. Daisie. Dandylion – sometimes thort to make you wet your bed.

I hear a faraway plane go over, the first I've heard since we've been here. And then I hear Frances, a yell announcing that she's woken, and doesn't know where the hell she is.

8 ∫

In a week, the panes of glass we brought from Mount Vernon are in the windows. (No putty – 'Why would I use putty on a log cabin Rita?' – instead Mick knocks nails half an inch into the logs while I hold the glass, then he goes indoors and does the same on the other side, and the nails miraculously hold the glass in place, but there are drafts, and gaps in some places. Rattly gaps, big enough for a mouse to slip in, or a bear to sneak its paw under.) Now the out-house has a door, a wooden one that Mick found under the deck and he teases, says 'the lady's honour has been preserved!'

He crawls about under the cabin, forcing a log-stump under the rotting bits to shore them up, then rolls out covered in grass and pine needles and writes 'chainsaw' on the 'Things we need' list. I sort out the junk around the cabin, throwing the cans in a black plastic bin-bag, the rotten clothes sprouting enormous wet mushroom growths in another; pulling up the dying heart-leaf arnica, chucking twigs and bits of logs on our scrap-pile for kindling. I wear rubber gloves to do this, which makes Mick laugh, and when I say 'There might be rattle snakes!' he laughs even more. 'Snakes would never come this far up the mountain,' he says. I write on the list 'bigger torch' and 'Colman fuel for the lamp'. Also, 'More nappies for Frances'. He sits next to me, takes the pen from me, writes 'More condoms'.

'There's loads left! I brought twenty boxes.'

At this he laughs, teasing again, bites my ear, says, 'Ah Rita, you love me really.'

I feel caught out, and giggle. Somehow the myth between us is that it's Mick who has the strongest sex drive, I'm just an enthusiastic amateur. Actually, we're getting through the Extra-Sensitive quicker than I thought. We're already on the second box.

'How we doing for money honey?' Mick asks, James Cagney voice. He's picking off some pine needles, sticking to his legs.

'Not bad, I counted it this morning. There's a thousand and twenty dollars left in the bag. We need to go into Goldtown again because I want to find out how to get a mailbox. Then Nicola can send me some money over.'

Frances has learnt a new word and has been saying it all week since our trip to Goldtown. 'Bi bi bi bit,' she says, and it's starting to irritate me. I don't know what the word is, but whenever she says it she gets her Sindy and hits her with the squeaky teddy and says to Sindy 'Bi, bit, bit!'

'Oh shut up, Frances, for God's sake,' I tell her. She looks at me in surprise.

'Why don't you take her off for a little wander? Do some exploring? I need to do some more banging this afternoon – I want to shore up the other side of the cabin and I have to bash the logs under with the hammer. It might be pretty noisy . . .'

Frances gives the blonde Sindy a resounding whack on the deck. 'Bit!' she squeaks.

I pop inside the cabin, grab my glasses, a T-shirt and the last Koala soda from the cool box. Then a T-shirt for Frances and her hat, then the *Book of Western Forests*, then my drawstring bag to put the lot in.

'OK,' I say, picking up Frances. 'Daddy!' she says. He kisses the hand she holds out to him.

'Go with Mummy. Go have a nice walk, Frankie. Daddy's doing some noisy banging, Frankie go with Mummy . . .'

'Bit, bit, bit,' says Frances.

I plant her down and tell her we're going for a walk. First we walk to the end of the drive, kicking aside the crushed pine cones. (I've worked out that crushed cones are a sign of a drive or road, don't know why I didn't think of this.) She toddles off in front of me, confident in her new trainers, a present from Mick's sister-in-law, which I've only just bothered to unpack. 'Nike-eee,' she says to herself, pausing to look at them, and then trotting off ahead.

I'm ravenous. I suppose it's about eleven in the morning – a guess as usual, based on the heat and the sun still being low in the east (I asked Mick in the end, pretending to have forgotten). It's hot enough to burn, and though we're both smothered in sun-lotion, reeking of coconut oil, I'm nervous about sunstroke. I pull Frances's stripy hat from my bag, tiptoe up behind her. While she's squatting to pull out a long, orangey-red trumpet-shaped flower among the grasses (Skyrocket, I looked it up) I drop the hat as lightly as I can onto her head.

No good, she feels it, flings it off and marches on.

I pick it up and follow – she's turning right at the bottom of our drive, onto the gravel road.

'Oh Frances, you have to wear your hat, you might get sunstroke with the sun on your head all the time . . .'

She ignores me, looks back over one shoulder, runs a little. I catch her up. Now she's stopping to look at droppings; dry pellets, bigger than sheep-droppings on the side of the gravel track. 'Deer,' I tell her. 'Deer-pooh.' She ignores me. She drops the Sindy, carries on walking. I pick it up and put it in my bag, a sorry naked creature, she looks like we do, with tangled fair hair, plastic skin smeared with dirt. We haven't had a bath in a week, just a cold basin wash, with the well water swished around a washing-up bowl. Frances's curls are in clumps at the back, the sun has made it white-blonde, she looks like a dandelion clock, a plant I've seen out here, although much bigger than the ones I know.

'Let's not stick to the road. A car might come.' I steer her into the trees, which she does happily, stopping to pick at the bark of one of them, and to dig her fingernails into a crusty piece of sap, and then sniff her fingers. I copy her and the smell is delicious; sweet, a resin. Benzoin, Mick says. 'Benzoin,' I tell her.

I try again with the hat, this time a direct approach, she's facing me, I squat down and place it firmly on her head. 'Come on now, Frances, I want you to wear this, we mustn't get ill out here, because what would we do?' But she scrunches her face into a cry, grabs the hat and hits me with it. It isn't a hard hit, it's only a child and a light cotton hat, but it catches me across my cheek and the annoyance I feel is shocking, sudden and stinging.

I whack her back, a stinging slap, hard across her leg. Her knees fold.

Screaming. She lies on the ground, wailing. Her cheek is wet and covered with dirt and pine needles.

'Oh Frances, shut up!' I say, surprised by the ferocity in my voice. I'm hungry, and too hot, and I'm furious with her.

'You never do what I say! Bloody child! Why can't you do what I say!' I yell, attempting to pick her up around her middle and plant her back on her feet, so that we can carry on walking. She freezes in my arms, turns stiff, makes her body impossible to pick up. Furious, I smack her again, this time across the stomach. She wails louder. Then I'm crying.

'Get up! I want to walk, you bloody child!' I yell again. Her face is red, her hair is clotted with little twigs, grasses. I drag her up by one arm. I try to get a grip on myself.

'Frances,' I try; a horrible, steely calm. 'Stop crying. Stand

up. You needn't wear your hat, but we're going for a walk.
You're getting filthy. Stand up. Here's your Sindy.'

I wipe my own tears with the back of my hand. I've no idea
why I'm crying. My hand smells like earth, and coconut oil,
and sweat. Frances stops crying and stands still. She takes the
Sindy, holding it by the hair. We walk in silence for a while,
come to a smallish rock, stuck in the middle of the trees, the
size of a small van, and lean against it. Moss grows on it in
patches, and ants run around the clumps of dark green. I
lift Frances up, and we sit on it, picking at the deep, soft,
satisfying moss with our fingernails. 'I'm sorry, Frances,' I
whisper. 'I don't know why I get so cross with you. *You*
haven't done anything. I need to try harder. I'm sorry.' I
look at her plump cheek in profile, her long spidery lashes
resting on skin so fine and perfect, like the skin of a fruit,
truly an English apple, a peach, with fresh smears of earth
on it. I love that cheek, those lashes, that nose. Why am I so
cruel? I brush at the earth with my hand and she twitches,
she dangles her legs. A creature flies past, I don't know what
it is, a locust or a kind of butterfly, making a snapping noise,
like clicking fingers. In the distance I can hear the sound of
Mick banging nails; regular, knock, knock, knock.

Frances taps the Sindy against the boulder, swinging her
by the hair. 'Bit, bit. *Bitch*,' she says.

# 9

Knock, knock, knock. I wake up. Something is tapping on the roof of the cabin. A hollow sound, a rap. Smart and quick. It's very early, it's cool and the light coming in is a pale, fresh butter yellow, but there *is* light, so I'm not scared. Frances and Mick are both sleeping. I slip my feet into the plimsolls beside the bed, open my glasses case and put them on. Knock, knock, knock. I pick up the notebook and pen, too. Then – an afterthought – I go back to the bed and kiss Mick once, swiftly and lightly on his arm outside the blankets, which is folded protectively across his chest.

It's a woodpecker of some kind, tapping on a tree nearest to the cabin. I stand very still, push my glasses onto my nose, the notebook into the waist of my leggings, and the pen behind my ear. I flick through the section in the book on birds, find it easily.

A Pileated Woodpecker, as big as a crow, mostly black and with a huge red crest, a white face and a kind of black eye-mask. I think about waking Mick – he would be impressed, it says here it is the largest woodpecker in America – but part of me wants to keep it for myself. The bird continues to tap with its beak while I carefully place the book on the ground, reaching for my notepad. But when I straighten up it hears me or sees the movement and takes flight, flapping away over the trees.

I jot down the details and a rough sketch. I'm glad it's light – otherwise I'd have thought twice about coming out on my own to see what the noise was. The land is beautiful at this time in the morning, peaceful, there's no breeze, the light is dazzling, exhilarating. The trees are more solid, the spindly branches are more spindly, the sky between them is an opaque, creamy blue, the shrubs and flowers hold their spines up.

Nights are different, in the night I feel differently. I can't sleep. At the squat it was Mick who couldn't sleep. He was always listening for burglars, or jumping out of bed and twitching at the curtain, thinking someone was trying to break into his car. Admittedly we were burgled twice, but that's par for the course in Dalston and that was before he put the enormous door on (he found it in a skip, it was like a warehouse door, took Mick and his mate Spider a whole afternoon to rig it to Spider's van and carry it back). Despite the burglaries, which anyhow both happened when we were out, I didn't worry about anyone breaking in, I worried about being trapped in the squat. Mick said, 'That's fine for you, you expect me to look after you.' But that wasn't true either. We argued about the door most nights. He wanted it locking, I wanted it unlocked. 'What if there's a fire and we need to escape quickly?' I said. That wasn't the real reason. I couldn't explain the real reason to Mick. I just needed desperately not to be locked in, and he needed just as desperately to lock things out.

Two weeks here and every night I'm nervy, although we shut the door and heave a log-stump in front of it. Even now the glass is in the windows I'm not reassured and anyway, I was right, there are cracks large enough to allow a tiny grey mouse with a black beady eye to run in under the glass, along a log, then away under the floorboards. If it's not the silence it's the noises. Rustlings, scamperings, scarperings. Sometimes loud sudden sounds, when a chipmunk knocks over a jar, or a packet of Cheerios it's been trying to get into. Sometimes an owl, not twitawoo like the story books but a dark, deep ppppprrrppp. Sometimes I hear what sounds like a faraway gun shot, just one, and then absolute silence where I hear my heart beat and my breathing and my blood in my veins.

Then it's the dreams. Dreams wake me. Then it's Frances, I hear Frances's little noises, squeaks and tiny cries in her sleep. I've rigged up a kind of mosquito net, it's a piece of lace curtain, pinned onto the corners of the travel cot with clothes pegs. If I brave the cold and pad over to her, undo the net to offer her some water in her bottle she just turns over again, dragging blankets with her, rolling the bottle into the corner of the travel cot. She looks like a hamster in a pen of cotton and netting.

Then it's the cold. My teeth chatter. My ribs feel too bony, each one clanks against the other, or against my wrists or forearms, if I clutch arms around my chest. Mick is like toast, I try to curve into his warmth, but he likes to move, fling his arms about. Sometimes he has dreams, much worse than mine, a roar will start up in him, I'm awake before it's peaked, he roars like someone on a rollercoaster, flying down to the bottom, but before this strange sound has crested I'm awake, saying 'Mick, Mick, it's all right, what is it? I'm here . . .'

In the morning if I ask him he never remembers; neither the dream nor the shouting, nor me patting him, calming him.

Mostly it's the fear. That's what it really is. I can hear every blade of grass tweaking, and I know something is out there. I hear twigs creak. I hear pattering feet. Sometimes hooves. I go through the *Book of Western Forests* in my head. Snow-shoe hare. A rabbit. A skunk. A deer. (Chewing at the deer brush. I know they like to feed at night.) Chipmunks. Squirrels. A raccoon. A porcupine. All perfectly harmless things, who live here, just like we do. Who would run a mile if I jumped out of bed and shined the torch on them. Who wouldn't come into the cabin, no. Not now that we've put all the perishables into the cool box with its tightly sealed blue plastic top. Not now that Mick has made a cabinet out of plyboard, a wooden nailed contraption with a flat plyboard lid which I weight – every night before I go to bed – with all my books. Creatures who wouldn't come in anyway, why would they? They can smell us. Our strange human smells of washing-up liquid and travel wash and mint toothpaste and disposable nappies.

The worst is when I lie with my bladder bursting. I go through it a hundred times. Mentally reach for the candles and matches we keep by the bed, light the candle, drip the wax, rest it on the saucer. Slip my feet into dusty plimsolls. Put on Mick's jumper. Patter over to the cabin door, hold the candle in one hand, push the door open with the other. I go through it again. Reach for the candle. Put my hand down beside the bed in pitch black. I go through it again. Reach . . . Listen. Silence.

My bladder is aching, my legs twisting and recrossing. I wake Mick, gently shaking his shoulder. 'Mick. Mick.'

'Huh?'

'Mick? Are you awake?'

'Uh, what, no I wasn't . . .'

He turns over, towards me. I can't see him.

'I need to go out. Are the matches on your side?'

He leans over me, rummages about on my side of the bed, has to reach right over to the floor. Then he props himself up on one elbow, lights the candle. The smell of wax as it drips onto the blanket. In the sudden flicker I can see his chin, his mouth grinning while he hands it to me.

'Stay awake while I go outside,' I say.

'Scaredy cat,' he whispers.

But he does, and I'm grateful, because the small strip of wobbly candlelight is nothing, we must get more batteries for the torch, that would be better. I shuffle slowly along, until my hand clutches the door handle, and I leave the cabin door open, and squat down just off the deck, in front of the truck, place the candle beside me where it flickers and lights up a thin dark trickle of water, forming a puddle on dry ground.

When I jump back into bed Mick pulls me to him. I shiver and giggle, feeling his breath in my ear, his erection prodding me in the stomach. I fling my whole body around him, legs and arms, an insect clinging to a twig.

In the morning Mick's run out of tobacco and suggests 'let's take Jim up on his offer and visit him and his "old lady" . . .'

'Get some smokes off Jim you mean,' I say, but it sounds good to me, we've been on our own for two weeks – we need some company. I brush my hair, check to see if there's dirt on my face in the wing-mirror of the truck, clean my glasses properly, with spit, and rummage through my case for a black and white dress that I haven't worn yet, a sleeveless shift dress with daisies all over it, a bit loud, but nice and cool in crisp cotton material, the only thing I possess that's ironed.

I've rigged up a line with rope between two Ponderosas and Frances's T-shirts, washed at Box Spring creek in the strange yellow water with the water-bugs ('Jesus Creepers', it says in the book; they can walk on water) are flapping there. The T-shirts and vests and knickers look surprisingly clean for a cold-water wash with washing-up liquid, and they smell wonderful, so I select a bright yellow T-shirt and stripy yellow and black shorts and yellow socks and blue jelly sandals. I attempt to comb her hair, but she hits out at me, wriggling off my knee. The knotted curls are impossible anyway. She scowls at me and runs into Mick's arms. 'Daddy's girl,' he says, scooping her up.

'Aren't you going to put a shirt on?' I ask.

'No, why should I? And what are you all dolled up for anyway?'

'I'm not!' I protest, climbing into the truck. We could walk but Mick wants to pick up an old oil barrel that Jim mentioned, he's going to have a go at making a stove, so that we don't have to have salad every night or use the tiny camping gas.

Mick straps Frances in, and I lean over her, saying: 'I don't want them to see this,' tickling his 'Cherie-Rose' tattoo through the hairs on his chest.

'Ah, jealous . . .' he teases, starting up the engine.

'Well, what will they think? We're not married anyway and you're sporting another woman's name . . .' I'm only half joking, my voice, I know, is plaintive.

'Tell them, if they ask, it's someone I loved very much, who died. Which is the truth.'

I open my mouth and close it, look at Mick, look at the tattoo and then back to the windscreen. It's the most he's ever said about the tattoo. It's the most I've ever asked him. He makes a skilful three-point turn in front of the cabin and pulls away down the driveway. I can't believe I've known Mick for nearly two and a half years and I didn't know that.

10

We drive a short distance on the gravel road, down the mountain until we come to the sign pinned on the trees, saying Nancy and Jim's Place. It's the house I saw on the first drive up Mount Coyote from Sinkalip. Mick turns in between two huge trees and we're on a kind of track, flattened grass and tyre marks, dotted with tree-stumps. We bump along it, with Frances protesting loudly every time we go over a small rock or snapped branch. I notice how much thinner the trees are here, and there are fewer of them, and the ground between trees is not messy like our snarl of shrubs; it's mostly short grass. Someone takes care of this bit of land, it's less of a wilderness.

Nancy and Jim's log cabin is surrounded by an assortment of car-parts, bikes, children and dogs. Smoke curls up from a chimney on the high roof. Their cabin is a different shape; tall and squashed where ours is low and square, and even I can see it's better made; the logs are stripped clean of bark and fit neatly together, the roof is a corrugated tin; the windows are made of some kind of polythene. The shape reminds me of the Old Woman who lived in a Shoe, higgledy piggledy, as if it has grown and evolved, things being added – extensions or back bedrooms.

The dogs come running and barking at our pick-up, three of them, giant dogs, like Huskies. Mick switches off the engine, takes out a paper to roll a spliff, then remembers he has neither tobacco nor grass, curses, and sticks the paper on the dashboard. I hesitate, my hand on the door handle.

'Go on, Rita, they're friendly.'

I carefully unstrap Frances, who is looking at the dogs and shouting 'Boo, boo!' trying to frighten them away. She looks worried, but determined, her round blue eyes fixed on their black noses, their open jaws and their yellow teeth, but she isn't crying. She's like me, I think, she'd rather die than admit she's scared.

'Here's Nancy,' Mick says, opening the door on his side, picking up the packet of Rizlas.

A woman in a long print skirt, with ginger hair tied back in a ponytail, is striding towards us, yelling at the dogs.

'Honey! Get back here. Alaska, Snake-Bite!'

She has hold of one by the scruff of the neck, she's holding out her other hand to Mick, the other two dogs have calmed down a bit, are growling softly, and hovering. I climb out my side, holding Frances.

'Mick – good to see you! Jim's out back, fixing the generator. And you must be Rita – hi, I'm Nancy . . .'

Her accent is soft, different from Jim's but I can't place it, State-wise – it might even be Canadian. She has freckles, far worse than mine, pale eye-lashes in a heart-shaped face, a wide mouth and wide hips and her navy-blue sweatshirt reads Jesus is My Lord. I smile at her, and since Frances is squirming in my arms, offer as an explanation, 'She's not used to dogs . . .'

'Oh these big old guys, they're real soft, they just look scary. Alaska now, she's part wolf, part husky, and that's her son, Honey, he's about the craziest, and Snake-Bite, she's his sister, she's a little skittish since she got bitten by a rattler . . .'

We're following her towards the cabin, she keeps her hand on the neck of Honey but the other two dogs have skulked off, uninterested, to be replaced by children; a tall boy of about eleven with brown hair down to his shoulders, a small red-headed girl, with the same colouring and solid build as Nancy, and a boy who looks just like her, except for being slightly bigger. He whizzes between the trees on his bike, waves once to us, then carries on.

'That's Clay. He's been ill with a flu bug and I only just let him out the house again,' Nancy laughs.

'No school today?' I ask the red-headed girl as she walks beside me, trying to touch Frances's feet in her jelly shoes.

'It's Saturday,' the child answers, and Nancy says: 'You guys are on Mount Coyote time, that's clear.'

Jim emerges from behind the cabin, grinning a wide grin and wiping his hands on his jeans.

'Hey! Mick, Rita! Good to see you guys, come the fuck on in . . .'

He looks delighted to see us; he and Mick immediately go into a huddle, with Mick – I suppose – explaining about his tobacco famine. They wander off together, deeper into the woods, Clay on his bike looping a figure of eight between them, and Nancy hmpphs and says, 'Jim's showing Mick his *crop*,' in a meaningful way which I feel I should understand, but don't.

I must look blank, because she continues, in a voice not even lowered for the kids: 'He's growing a whole crop of grass. Skunk weed. A few of the guys up here do it, but you know? There are these incentive schemes the police have been promoting – turn someone in today and make five hundred bucks. That's what happened to the guys who owned your place. That's why they sold it so cheap. I don't like it. We have a lot a friends up here but there's always someone who'll turn you in for a few bucks.'

We're packed into the tiny kitchen, me, Frances, the little girl, and the older boy. The other boy, Clay, went with Mick and Jim. Their log cabin is all nooks and crannies, and every space filled. The polythene window casts a faint grey light, there are patchwork curtains and tea-towels and home-made oven gloves; every corner is stuffed with food, with jars and packets; Mary Lu biscuits, Paul Newman salad dressing, Aunt Jemima's Pancake Mix and enormous bottles of Pepsi and cranberry juice. Each inch of wall space (log) has a child's picture pinned to it, a photograph or a postcard. It smells of dogs and coffee and cedar and cigarette smoke and something spicy, which simmers in a pan on Nancy's oven.

Nancy hands me a coffee, poured from a pot she took off the top of her stove. She has two ovens; one that looks normal, a range fuelled by a gas bottle which she tells me she gets filled at the store, and a massive barrel-shaped stove, a grey, sideways barrel, which has logs inside it and a chimney producing the smoke we saw as we drove up. She has an enormous pan of water heating up on it, and tells Frances to mind it, it 'gets real hot'.

'This is amazing, it's so cosy in here,' I say, my glasses steaming up from the coffee.

'Your place is pretty cold when the sun goes down, huh?'

I laugh in agreement. Frances has wriggled off my knee and discovered one of the dogs, trying to nap at the bottom of a makeshift log ladder to the upstairs. She is still scared, but now she's trying to provoke the dog, she is prodding him with the Sindy, poking him just under the ear, then screeching a little and running away, then poking him again. I watch her out of the corner of my eye, trying to follow the conversation with Nancy, but acutely aware of Frances.

'You intend to stay the winter? You have to insulate the logs, you know?'

She starts telling me all the various ways to do this, the cheap ways and the expensive ways, newspaper or plaster and chicken wire and she manages to do this despite interruptions; demands for a drink from Katie, the littlest, an argument to sort out between them. I interrupt too, eventually, to ask in a voice that comes out small and worried: 'How cold does it get up here in winter?'

'Oh, you know. Most years we're snowed in completely for at least two weeks.'

She points to a photo, pinned to a log above her head and curling around the edges with the steam from the cooking, 'That's nineteen seventy-nine, the year we came up here. I was pregnant with Randy. He was nearly born in the pick-up on the way to the hospital at Sinkalip. That was a pretty deep-snow year.'

I stare at the picture of Nancy, twelve years younger, in a red jumper with thin legs, round as a fat robin in front of a cabin with snow packed on the roof, thick on the ground and weighting the trees. A picture of the door on the squat in Dalston flashes into my head, that big, ugly door that Mick wanted locked all the time. I see it suddenly deep in snow, snow up to the lock, the squat in snow, snow blanking the windows, immersed in snow, like being inside a giant white wedding cake. Nancy is saying, 'I grew up in Canada so I guess I'm used to snow! The school bus can't get up here and you need the plough to get out. You have chains for your truck?' and it takes me a while to answer, I'm somewhere else, at the squat, the kitchen is so hot my palms are sweating and my head feels like it might burst.

'I don't know, I'd better ask Mick – *Frances*! For God's sake, leave that poor dog alone.'

I must have shouted really loud because Frances bursts into tears and Nancy visibly jumps. I'm embarrassed but I can't control myself; I grab Frances roughly, she tries to cling to the ladder and I have to peel her fingers off one by one. I grit my teeth. The feeling I'm about to burst is pushing in my ribs, I don't know why I'm so angry, so suddenly, but there's no doubt about it, I am.

'Frances. Stop screaming,' I tell her, through my teeth.

Nancy looks round from the stove, where she has been stirring something spicy, a sauce, in an enormous pan. I feel Nancy's eyes on me but I daren't look up. Every ounce of my energy is going into controlling the desire to smack Frances, to smack her hard, to shut her up.

Nancy seems to hesitate, turns back to the stove, then says to her son, who had been running in and out through the open cabin door, 'Clay honey . . . can you find a little bike for the baby? You kids go play outside and take the baby with you.'

'Here, I'll hand her to them,' Nancy says, holding arms out for the squealing, red-faced, damp bundle of fury which is Frances in a tantrum. Frances chooses that moment to dig her nails into my arm, and now it is me who shrieks and practically drops her. I hand her to Nancy with relief. Not that I expect her to fare any better and she doesn't; Frances continues to wail and to screw up her face and make her body stiff and impossible to hold, until Nancy puts her down, hands her a cracker and Clay pulls on her hand. Katie and Randy jump up, follow Clay outside.

Nancy and I are silent for a moment. I look down at my arm, rub the spot where Frances pinched me, pick up my coffee cup, sip the last dregs. My temples ache, a rushing feeling which threatens tears.

'Can I get you a refill?' Nancy offers, holding her hand out for the coffee cup.

'Thanks,' I say. My voice comes out clogged, so I clear it and try again. 'Thanks a lot. This is really nice coffee.'

'I love your accent,' says Nancy, handing me the filled cup.

# 11

I sip my coffee until I hear Mick and Jim coming back, talking loudly, and I stand at the open cabin door, watching Jim bending to lift a flat wooden slat off the ground near our truck, revealing a fridge with a red door, sunken into a deep hole.

'Where d'you get your power from?' I say and Jim laughs. A long pause while he takes two cans of Coors from the packed fridge, then he answers smilingly: 'City girl. The only power we have is from that genny and it ain't on right now.' Seeing that I still don't get it, he adds: 'If you sink something in the ground it's insulated, you know? Stays cool.'

Jim is wearing the same checked shirt and jeans but today he has trainers on and ridiculous sun-glasses which make me feel sorry for him; purple reflective shades, as if he's trying to look cool himself. I see my own freckly face, a flash of blonde fuzz surrounding it; I know he is looking at me although I can't see his eyes and I stand in the doorway, watching Frances riding a trike with Katie and Clay helping to push her.

'Hey, Rita, need a beer?'

'Yes, thanks, I'd love one.'

He fetches a third Coors for me and I place my coffee cup back on the draining board next to Nancy and step outside.

'Look what Jim gave me,' says Mick, excitedly. His pupils are wide so I know they tucked into the skunk weed, but what he's holding out isn't that, it's a round metal pan with a grid at the bottom – a kind of flat colander.

'What is it?' I ask. Just outside the cabin there's an old picnic table and some benches where Jim and Mick are sitting, so I open my can of Coors and sit with them, examine the colander-type object without a clue.

'It needs cleaning up,' mumbles Jim. 'It's nothing. Two dollars ninety-seven at Hank's Hardware. It's for gold panning.'

'Oh!'

'Jim's going to show me a good spot at the river in Sinkalip. For panning. And if there's gold in the river there might be gold in the rocks.' Mick shows me the gold panning movement, shaking the pan in a shuffling and tipping action, laughing at himself. 'Rita,' he goes on, 'Jim's told me how to get a licence to buy dynamite and it's easy, we just have to go into Omak with my driving licence and apply . . .'

'Good, great,' I mutter. I see that they have tied the empty oil barrel, an old rusty thing, onto the bed of the pick-up, and I'm wondering how it will ever be an oven like Nancy's oven; it's hard to imagine.

Jim sits opposite me and Mick, I find myself staring at his astonishing frazzled beard and hair, in this bright sunlight I notice more grey than last time, but also streaks of gold. In response to my staring he says, 'Your old man's growing a beard so's he can look the part on Mount Coyote . . .' and leans over the table to tug at the bit of a goatee Mick is growing. Mick laughs and rubs the growth himself, Jim booms, 'You have a fuckin' great old man. Fuckin' great.' He tries hugging Mick, across the table, making Mick laugh again and nearly fall off the picnic bench. I sip my Coors and push my glasses onto my nose, then glance over at Frances, who is ramming her bike into whoever gets in front of it; Katie, another dog . . . 'Not like that,'

Clay keeps saying, but when she rams Katie's ankles, he laughs.

'Frankie!' Mick yells over, following my gaze. 'Play nice now . . .'

'I had older brothers like Katie,' I tell them.

'That's why you're such a tough cookie,' Mick tells me, kissing the top of my bare arm. He's in his puppy dog mood, another sign that he's been smoking grass.

He and Jim go through the cigarette ritual using Jim's tobacco and papers and another bag of skunk weed mysteriously produced from the back pocket of Mick's shorts. They tap the ash into an empty can at the table. The smell of strong herby grass wafts over us. When Jim offers it I shake my head but for the first time I'm tempted, if I knew how to smoke I'd say yes.

'You're like Nancy, huh, no vices, Rita? No swearing, no smoking, no drinking to excess?'

'Oh, she swears all right. She swears like a trooper!' Mick says, his English colonel accent. He laughs, snuggling up to me on the picnic bench and digging me in the ribs with his hand.

'And I drink too,' I offer, waving the Coors at them.

'Nancy don't. Don't drink, don't smoke, don't swear. How the fuck does she put up with me?' Jim cracks up laughing and Nancy hears him from the kitchen, calls out, 'I hear you Jim Shaughnessy. The Lord gives me strength, that's the truth.'

Mick and I exchange glances; religion embarrasses us. Jim is more jovial than ever, laughs again, fetches three more beers and slamming them down on the table says: 'Stay and have lunch you guys. Smokey brought us a deer he shot last night. A peace offering. I fixed my truck' – he waves his arm in the direction of the pick-up – 'and my teeth. Had to use half of Nancy's savings for the fuckin' teeth. How come you guys have such good fuckin' teeth? You wealthy or something?'

'Oh no, I'm on the dole . . . it's free in England, if you're unemployed.'

'Is that right?' He shoves the Coors over to me. 'Whatever. Stay for lunch. We have plenty. Ain't that right Nancy?'

She steps out into the sun-light, handing out Graham crackers to the children nearest the cabin door.

'Oh sure,' she replies warmly. I suspect Jim caught her off-guard making offers on her behalf with no effort to help her, but if he did, she gives no sign.

'Can I help you?' I say, dutifully. The beer makes me lazy, Frances is taken care of and somehow I don't want to think about my show of bad temper in the kitchen, I'd much rather sit out here in the sun, enjoying the banter with Jim and Mick. With the boys.

Nancy wipes her forehead with the back of her hand and smiles. 'You know, I don't know what to do with this deer. Come see, maybe you'd like to take some, Rita? It's a doe, we can't eat all of it right now . . .'

'Oh no,' I say in alarm, 'we haven't got an oven—'

'— yet!' interjects Mick, waving towards the oil barrel.

'— or a fridge. I mean, like yours.'

'Venison is good,' Jim tells us. 'Tender. You'll love it.'

'I – I wouldn't know what to do with it?'

'What are you, some kinda vegetarian?' he asks.

I stand up, pulling the black daisy dress down, aware suddenly of how naked Mick and I seem, compared to Jim and Nancy in their long-sleeved shirts. It must be ninety degrees at the minimum – why aren't they sweltering?

'No, I, uhhm . . .' I trot off after Nancy back to the kitchen and as I leave I overhear Jim: 'I was. A fuckin' vegetarian. Then when we came up here, I thought: God gave us all these fuckin' creatures to eat. What else are they here for? You can live simply up here, but you have to eat. I mean, I'll shut the fuck up if I'm wrong, but nature's mean. I can't stand these vegetarian types who think it's all cute little puppy dogs and

Bambi and don't want to know about the real world . . . yeah
– what do I know? I'll shut the fuck up . . .'

I follow Nancy into the kitchen but there she is just picking
up a knife, a huge knife, hung up on a hook stuck in a log,
high out of the kids' reach.

'I haven't done a thing with it yet, it won't be ready now
for a while . . .'

She goes to the back of the cabin, to a little construction
made of logs, which I'd thought an hour ago was the
out-house, until I'd tried the door and realised that it
appeared to be full of more logs, chopped ones. Then I
saw the actual out-house, quite a bit smaller and sensibly
further away from the cabin. In this shed, there is a pile
of neatly stacked chopped logs, the blond semi-circle ends
facing outwards, and a table. On the table a sheet of grey
plastic, and on that, a lump the size of an eleven-year-old
boy, covered in another piece of bloodstained grey plastic.

Flies buzz around and Nancy swats at them, chatting away:
'Smokey brought it couple a hours ago. Just caught it, this
morning, says she was on his property – a doe and her young,
a young buck. I'd better do something fast, you know, get
most of her into the refrigerator. It'll be fine when Jim gets
through a rack of Coors, then there'll be some room in
there . . .'

There is a weird smell and I know I know that smell,
although it isn't strong, and it isn't the smell of meat. I stand
near the blooded lump dreading Nancy lifting the plastic and
trying to work out a way to protest that I can't possibly help
her, and the smell gets right into my nostrils and I close my
eyes for a second and swallow and taste nausea, tight and
acid in the back of my throat.

'I can't look!' I rush out from under the logs. I don't care
what she thinks. The smell, stronger than ever, a sweet-stink
animal smell. It's the smell Frances had, when she was born,
at the moment they handed her to me in the hospital, before

they cleaned her up, a smell of blood and smeary mucus. I thought only birth smelled like that. My hand goes up to my nose, to my glasses. I take long deep breaths of the smoky pine air.

## 12

But in the end it isn't me who is sick, it's Mick, and it's not the venison which does it, it's the drink and the skunk weed. He has to mooch off to some trees at the furthest end of their drive; I'm helping Nancy clear up in the kitchen, lifting the hot water from the pan on the stove to the washing-up bowl, and I see Mick through the window, doubled up.

'It's probably time we were going. Thanks for the meal Nancy, it's been really lovely . . .'

'You guys have a flash-light with you? Let me get you one – it's nearly dark . . .'

Frances has a battered toy raccoon that Katie gave her, a bottle full of Kool-Aid and some M&Ms, smearing her face with red and green, so she looks contented, sitting on the trike near the cabin door, big eyes staring at me over her bottle. I gather up our other bits and bobs; Mick's newly aquired Top tobacco from the picnic bench, Frances's discarded blue jelly shoes and socks, and put them in the truck, then I go over to Mick, leaning his forehead against a tree.

'Are you all right?'

'Huh. Uh. Fine.'

'Think you can drive? I – we should probably be going . . .'

'Yeah. Sure. I'm sober. It's just the—'

'The grass Jim gave you. I think it's strong you know, Mick.

Stronger than you're used to. Or else it was the deer-meat, I'm glad I didn't have any . . .'

He groans, straightens up, attempts a wobbly stride over to the pick-up. I yell out goodbye and thanks again and decide Frances needs a quick nappy-change, so lie her on my side of the seat, wobble the torch over her so that there's enough light to stick a fresh Huggy on her, and chuck the warm sodden plastic lump of the old nappy in the back.

Mick is staring straight ahead. I hand him the torch to light up the ignition and he tries to put the key in. Nancy is rounding up the children, bikes and dogs, Jim is still nursing a can of Coors at the picnic table when we finally get the engine started. Mick reverses, hits a stump, jerks forward, stalls, reverses again, and we pull away. Four hundred yards down the track, he stops, opens the truck door and vomits out onto the grass.

Frances, charmed, gives a wonderful impression of the sounds Mick is making. 'Daddy – yuuuughhh,' she says, bouncing in her seat. Silence from Mick. He pulls himself back in, slumps onto the wheel.

'Mick, are you OK?'

No reply. I stare at his shoulders in panic, gently shake them.

'Rita. I think you'll have to drive,' he groans, from under his arms.

'Oh God. How? I can't . . .'

'It's not far. It's a couple of miles, three at the most. There won't be another car on the road. I'll talk you through it.'

'But I've never driven in my life, I haven't got the first idea . . .'

'You'll be – fine.'

He opens his door, gets out, wipes his mouth with the back of his hand, comes round to my side. I'm rooted to my seat, clutching the torch.

'Mick, I don't know . . .'

'Come on, what else can we do?'

'We could walk.'

'The oil barrel's in the back. I want to take it home. Tonight.'

'We could go back and ask Jim to drive us.'

'Have you seen the state Jim's in? He's worse than me . . .'

'Nancy then? Maybe Nancy drives? I'm sure she said she did.'

'Rita. I feel very sick. I am going to be sick again in a minute. My head is throbbing. Get out of the pick-up, turn the key in the ignition and put the fucking thing in drive!'

That tone of voice. I climb out, uncertainly. We're still close enough to hear voices from Jim and Nancy's and a dog barking, but other than that, I've no idea where we are. It isn't pitch black yet but it's growing darker by the minute, and there's no moon, only faint shadowy trees and the sound of cracking cones as Mick steps on one, climbing into my side.

I'm shaking as I turn the key and feel the engine vibrating beneath us. Mick puts on the lights and the trees in front jump out – yellow, sudden, poised. Mick drops his head into his hands for a moment and I wait, hands trembling on the wheel.

'Push the gear lever into drive. Let the handbrake off, keep your foot steady on the gas. There's no clutch, so don't worry about that.'

My shoulders feel like a yoke across my back. I strain my eyes through my glasses, clutching the steering wheel so tightly that my arms are as rigid as branches, I'm peering forward, feeling the truck pull away – too quickly – so I'm trying to slow it with the brake and at the same time do something about the steering which is all over the place. Mick isn't even watching, his face is in his hands, I'm not sure if it's through sickness or dread, but I squeak at him, 'What now, what now?' and he manages to grunt, 'Turn left at the end here, that's the road,' and I can't believe how I can feel every stone and cone beneath the tyres, how come I never felt this when I was a passenger?

Turning onto the gravel road I can't see much more, only the first few yards, illuminated by the truck lights. Sweat is making the steering wheel hard to grip and the road itself is slippery, I can't send the wheels where I want them to, and when I steer to avoid some hole or big stone, we go over it anyway. Mick curses every time I jolt him. Trees keep looming up in front of us, too close to the bonnet – a swerve from me and they leap back to the side of the road. The truck chugs and bucks, and I try to reign it in, pull it over, keep some sort of control. I'm rigid with concentration and when Mick says 'left here, here we are –' I'm startled, he bursts in on the sound of the engine vibrating inside me, and under me, in my foot and up the muscles of my leg – he is somewhere far away.

We rattle and bump down the drive towards our cabin and swerve to a screeching halt, just short of it. Mick leans over to put the handbrake on and pull the gear lever into neutral, grins briefly at me, then switches off the key. When he turns off the lights the windscreen in front of me is pitch black, I'm tucked safely inside, smiling and staring at black glass, with not a tree, a rock, a cabin, or a star in sight.

Falling asleep, later, I think about Mick not getting mad. I'd thought he would get mad, I felt the beginning of him getting mad, but he didn't. I drove, I got us home, in the middle of the woods. Mick didn't get mad.

He didn't get mad this time because I drove. He's been angry out here because of all the driving he's had to do, he hates it when I'm too dependent, too needy, like I was when Frances was first born. He loves me because I'm strong, I am strong, I'm stronger than him. I can be strong out here for all of us, things will work out. I just need to be stronger. I fall asleep wearing the daisy dress, to the sound, very far away, of howling dogs, or maybe it's something else, wild dogs, coyote, wolves even? I must ask Mick, Mick will know, I'll ask Mick in the morning.

## 13

'Yeah, coyotes. That's what they'll be.'

Mick is lying on his stomach on the deck, his head in the oil barrel, an assortment of tools scattered around him. First, he tried cleaning it with a wire brush – a patchy success. Now he is cutting a little door into it, and the door must have a 'baffle' he tells me, to regulate the flow of air. A book called *How to make an oil-barrel stove by Old Wik*, lies open on the deck beside him, flecked with dust and metal shavings.

'How come you never hear them? They were so loud last night, like howling and then yapping and then another lot seemed to be replying; not just for five minutes, it went on for ages. You and Frances slept through the lot.'

'I suppose it isn't called Mount Coyote for nothing, eh?'

Mick carefully pulls his head out of the oil barrel. He has cut a metal square from the barrel and brings this with him, taking off his T-shirt and using it to wipe the metal square.

Frances loves anything she thinks is Mick's, especially the tools. The second he puts the cutters down she makes a grab for them, but he gets there first, laughs, swings them high out of reach, says, 'Not so fast, baby!' Seeing her face curl up he gives her a 'knockknock' (hammer) and a handful of nails ('Precious these, Frankie, don't lose them . . .') and lets her try knocking them into the planks of wood on the deck. He holds his hand over her fat fingers as they struggle to hold the nail. She raises the hammer.

'Not so high! You're going to hurt your fingers.' Mick takes the nail from her hand and shows her again, swapping the hammer he gave her for a smaller one, and showing her how to raise it only an inch from the nail. I bite my tongue, convinced she'll smash her finger. After a few misses, she manages to hit the nail, wonkily, and beams her pleasure up to Daddy.

'See. You were going to tell me not to give her that, weren't you?'

'No,' I say.

'Not everyone is like you, Rita. She obviously takes after me, she's practical.'

'Well, maybe my Dad was never around to show me how to do anything practical. And when he *was* around he would never let me touch his tools.'

'I should think not!' Mick grins, rolling over on his back to wink up at me and run his hand up my leg. 'Knockknock!' yells Frances, meaning: Show me again! Give me some more nails!

I'm still full of my driving success and a sense that for once, I didn't make a fool of myself, didn't make Mick mad by letting him down. Whistling, I go inside to read up on the coyotes.

I thought Mount Coyote was an Indian – I mean, Native American – name, I'm reading up on stuff like that. I have a book of Coyote stories by a woman from the Colville reservation: Mourning Dove. Coyote, the spirit-creature is small and vain and foolish but he always triumphs in the end, outwitting more powerful beings through stealth and trickery. There are loads of stories about him and they all relate to this area, naming landmarks like the Big Chop mountains nearby and Top Lake. I prefer thinking that the mountain is named after this Coyote rather than the one that Mick means.

'Coyote: the best runner among the canids, the Coyote can leap 14 feet and cruises normally at 25–30 mph, up to 40 mph for short distances . . .'

But maybe they are one and the same thing? In my dreams last night something came flying through the windows of the cabin, whirring, whipping up shorts and tea-towels, a motor running, a cross between the truck I was driving and a wild creature.

Road-runner and Wiley Coyote rolled into one. Lucky bloody Mick and Frances to sleep so soundly; all the noises outside, the clamorous ones like the coyote cries and the tiny ones like twigs cracking, infiltrate my dreams, mix up with them, so that the whole night is one long turmoil, swimming in and out of sleep.

'They're nothing to worry about, Rita, you know.'

Mick is in the cabin beside me, taking the book from me and looking at it himself.

'They're just wild dogs. They'd never come anywhere near us, I mean, we don't even have chickens. Even if they did come outside to scavenge, they wouldn't come in the cabin, why would they? Are you really worried?'

He asks as if it's occurred to him for the first time. I close the book.

'No, I s'pose not. It's just at night. My sleep is so disturbed. I feel in this heightened state of – something or other. As soon as I lie down my heartbeat quickens.'

'Ah. And I thought it was the nearness of my gorgeous body.'

I'm glad to change the subject. 'Oh it is. It is,' I murmur, giving his chest a kiss, taking my face down to his belly button. The hairs on his chest tickle my nose and his skin smells of metal shavings. For a full minute I breathe him in, wrap my arms around him to press his body to my face. Mick's size, his strength, the taut solid flesh of his stomach, the curving muscles on his arms, his heat, the scent of him, the soft fur on his chest, sometimes these things make me feel blissfully small and safe, like a baby in the middle of a deep forest . . .

'Daddy, knockknock!' says Frances, at the doorway. She's lost all the nails and holds out her hand, wanting more.

It's a week before we go on the gold-panning expedition Mick is longing for. He finishes the oil-barrel stove, we buy a chimney in two parts from Hank's Hardware and after some filing and struggling Mick fits this on; then there's a trip up to the roof with me holding the ladder while it all slots into place. Luckily there is already a hole where the other chimney used to be; we even find bits of it stuffed under the cabin, too rusty and bent to be of use. I call it the bell-end chimney and Mick says that's typical of me, calls me a 'Rude goil' in his Irish accent. But the first meal on our new stove is delicious! With chopped up Ponderosa crackling in the barrel we put pans of potatoes, sweetcorn and freshly podded peas on the top to boil, and in another flat pan Mick fries pork chops, onions and tomatoes. It takes ages but it's the best meal we've had in weeks; everything fresh and crunchy and with a faint taste of smoky wood.

We jump in the truck and then I jump out again to gather various things together; gold-pan, map, the usual nappies, bottle of juice, sun-cream and sun-hat, towel in case I want to swim, soap, toothbrush in case there's the opportunity to have a wash, spare set of clothes for Frances in case she gets too wet, glasses case for me so I can take them off safely, twenty dollars in cash for petrol, three green apples. Eventually I can't think of anything else and Mick has checked the oil and water so we set off. Blue sky, clouds like brush strokes above the trees. A chipmunk chipping away and a blue jay squawking. As the truck pulls down the drive I look back at the cabin and think: that's ours. It's real, all this is real, the long strands of fireweed, some small birds making the red Indian paintbrush flicker among the other grasses as we bounce along the track near Box Spring. No matter how hard I try, I can't fully picture anywhere else. London is disappearing. Dalston. The grey and the brown of Dalston. Red plastic seats, the kind that stick out at bus stops like little square tongues, too hard to actually sit on. Dalston has been replaced by trees and sky and now that we are driving down the mountain, a dusty road with bunches of quail and – now – a ruffed grouse with her fat brown chest puffed out, agitated, trying to hurry her chicks across the road before we approach her.

I feel as if I've reached the top of something and bubbled over the sides, like a pan of hot milk. If Mick spoke to me now, I'd burst into tears.

We drive down the mountain singing at the top of our voices, along with the tape-player; 'Brass in pocket' by Chrissie Hynde. We pass two trucks; one we recognise as belonging to Buster, a friend of Jim's, so we wave, and Frances calls her new word: 'Howdee, howdee!'

The colours, the lush green pine trees, the crusty brown-grey of the bark, seep in through my pores; even if I close my eyes now I can feel them and see them; I no longer bother to point out things to Frances; the chicken hawk overhead with the red-gold under its wings, the marmot sitting up on its back legs, holding its paws up to its chest like a dog begging – I know she notices these things, know that her eyes widen, her head twists to follow as we drive past.

Over the summit and the fields turn liquid; long, honey-coloured grasses and sage-brush on one side, a stand of Quaking Aspen on the other, the white bark pitted with strange black marks, like Egyptian eyes. The leaves wave on stalks so light that the entire tree really does appear to quake. Where is Dalston now? Where's Arcola Street, with it's high-walled sweat-factories, the haunting smells of Turkish Ocsabasi cafés among the broken glass and dog shit, the police sirens, the guy standing under my window ten nights in a row with a brick, calling 'slag' up to his sister next door, Delroy who makes my heart ache to look at him: ten years old and bright as a button, spending six weeks every summer hanging around the streets, swinging his skinny arms . . .? I'm filled with such a rush that when on the next track, Chrissie welcomes her baby to the human race with its war, disease and brutality, I do spill over, tears tipping down my face.

*My baby, my lover, my family, my tree, my fireweed, my pine cone, my blade of grass, my land, my home: mine, mine, mine.*

## 14

After the stand of Quaking Aspen we're in the valley. Now
there are fruit trees, in neat rows, props holding the heavy
branches and each like a story-book tree, laden with shiny
red apples, then peaches. The smell of warm apples drifts in
on the dust through the windows, and a small plane flies
low, crop spraying.

'They look nearly ready,' Mick says, 'I can get some
work fruit picking. D'you think the money will hold out
until then?'

Mick likes me to have charge of the money, counting it,
keeping the dollars folded in an old make-up bag under the
bed, selecting how much is needed for every shopping trip.

'We could call in at Goldtown and check our mailbox.
Nicola might have sent the last of my dole over. She doesn't
dare sign on any longer for me, she said that was the limit
in her last letter.'

We have a key and a mailbox in Goldtown's post office,
bought for only a few dollars, number 1789, already we
have junk mail appearing in there; newsletters about Hank's
Hardware and onions from Walla Walla, six for a dollar at
Thrifty's Summer Sale.

The orchards are replaced by houses, first the flimsy flat
houses of the Mexican workers then the bigger, white-
painted wooden houses with sprawling gardens, parked up

with the RVs and motorbikes belonging to the wealthier inhabitants of Goldtown. I resist the temptation to ask Mick to stop at a moving sale and instead he parks outside the post office and I swing through the doors into the huge, shiny-clean room with its rows of locked drawers, the strong floor-polish smell. I check ours but find nothing.

Then it's a drive through town and out in a direction we haven't taken before. We're heading for the Sinkalip river, and Mick drives towards the Big Chop mountain range, named after an Indian princess who was, I read, transported there by a suitor and lived unhappily, pining for her family; passing a huge golf course with the most amazing mountain views, and old men trundling around in motorised cars with their golf clubs; then through Nighthawk – Nighthawk Welcomes the Class of Sixty-Two – with directions underneath for a summer reunion party. We whisk through the town in a matter of minutes, and we're out the other side, in a flat valley of mostly ranches – massive fields and massive cows, brown and white, patchy, horned, wild-looking cows, nothing like a dainty English Friesian.

'Nighthawk has a gold-rush past as well,' Mick says. 'It's in that book about the Klondike Jim was showing me. Gold and silver. There's plenty of mines still there, apparently.'

As if to prove his point, one suddenly appears in the field we're driving beside. Mick screeches to a halt and points it out to me. In a field of bumpy grass, there is one raised bump about the size of a garden shed, overgrown with grass but with a visible door in it and a sign propped up against it. 'Keep out. Danger. Private Property.'

'Fancy a look?' he offers. I shake my head. He continues driving, the gold pan rattling in the back, Frances getting restless in the front, Mick singing the theme tune to the *Beverley Hillbillies*, in his best hillbilly voice.

'Come listen to a story about a man named Jed, a poor mountaineer, barely kept his family fed, and then one day as he was shootin' at some food, up from the ground came a bubblin' crude. Oil that is. Black gold . . .'

The river is wide, fast flowing but shallow in the place where we stop, surging over the stones, and the edges full of marshy weeds.

'How do we know where to look?' I ask Mick, lifting Frances out of the car and taking off her socks and putting her jelly shoes back on without them.

'A bend in the river is best. That way the gold can collect there. Jim told me about this place, says it might be promising . . .'

'You can go in,' I tell Frances, 'but just here, by the edge.'

'Shooose,' she says.

'Yes, in your shoes, that's OK, they're plastic shoes, for going in water.'

Mick takes her hand, places a foot gingerly onto a large flat rock, lifts Frances onto it, and stands beside her. Now the river flows around them and I'm still on the bank, with the gold pan.

'Pass us the pan, Rita.'

I step from the soft reedy earth of the bank to the cold water. The bottom of the river feels silty and sinks under my feet, the water splashes up just over my ankles. I hand Mick the pan and then stay where I am, resting my hands on the top of my knees, bending over, staring into the river.

'It's so clean. I can see little fishes. Look, Frances, look at this!' Mick lifts her to the edge of the rock they're standing on, and squatting down she can see the shoal of thumb-sized fish. She squeals excitedly as a huge purple dragonfly flies past her, tries to grab at it. There are loads of these; their bright purple and yellow tails flit over the surface of the river like sparks from a fire. Mick has the pan and is now knee-deep, further out into the river, shuffling the pan along the river-bed.

'Isn't it flowing a bit fast? I mean, won't the gold get moved along, if there is any?'

'Gold is nineteen times heavier than water. It sinks to the bottom.'

Mick lifts the pan out of the water, shakes it, and carefully tips the silty water off the top. He examines what's left for ages, he is standing looking at it for so long, that I start wading over to him, leaving Frances dangling her legs from the rock.

'Anyhow, Mick, what does gold look like?'

'You can't be serious!'

'I mean, does it look different? In its raw state?'

We both stare into the pan. Mick gently nudges tiny stones around with his finger, and waits until the dust clouding the water settles.

'Native gold is much duller. But it's still gold, you can see that. It's kind of gnarled-up looking. As if it's been chewed on. It's usually found as part of quartz rock so if you can find quartz there might be a chance of finding gold. And it will be in tiny amounts, but that doesn't matter, it's finding any at all that matters. Any at all, means there may be more.'

He tilts the pan, holding it to the light, to see if the sun will bounce off its contents. The dragonflies sticking to reeds above the river are the only things that glitter; those and the buckles on Frances's shoes. Mick plunges the pan into the river again, and I stride back through the water, deciding to get the soap from the truck and give Frances a wash.

There is a silty taste on my tongue. The river smells of earth. I pause, trying to breathe in more of the clean earth smell, and when I lift my head up from staring at the water and push my glasses back on my nose, I suddenly realise I have been staring at a frog, a huge, yellow-eyed frog. A grey, ugly frog, no, it's probably a toad; raised black bumps on its back and glittering eyes, too big to miss – but I did miss it – and when I blink, look away, as if released from my stare, the toad moves slightly.

Western Toad, Mick says it is. Common round here. Jim has them in his well. The Wild-Western Toad, I rename it – kiss this and you wouldn't get a prince, you'd get a cowboy. Which is fine by me.

Driving back, Mick is quiet. I know he is disappointed, but Frances and me are happy. Her newly washed hair is almost dry and sticks out in a blonde fluff around her head. She has learned three new words; toad, soap and daccon-fye (dragonfly). She says these quietly to herself, and then 'dink' and I pass her some juice in her bottle, basking in the sun through the truck window, my skin still tingling just below the surface, from the cold river.

'You don't fucking care anyway.'

'What?'

Still, my mood is fine, I've no idea, even from the tone of Mick's voice, what's coming, what could possibly be coming, today, this day; the day when I feel at long last, that we are a happy family, that we made the right decision, that I am a good mother, that I love Mick and everything has turned out right.

'You think it's one big fucking joke.'

'Mick, what's this about? I don't know what you're on about. And can you stop swearing, in front of Frances?'

I'm trying to keep the school-mistress out of my tone, and I wish I hadn't said the last bit, knowing how much it will annoy him, but I can't help it. When Mick swears Frances gets edgy. She rolls her big eyes from me to Mick and then back again. She holds the teat of her bottle in her mouth, but stops sucking.

'You don't think we'll find any gold. You're not interested in what I want.'

'I do, I'd love to, who in their right mind wouldn't want to find gold? Of course I do.'

My heartbeat has quickened, and I sit very still, listening to it, waiting for it to calm down, to go back to normal. Silence from Mick. I'm absolutely stock-still, I'm like the toad; the trick is, not to move. Stay frozen and Mick will come back from wherever he is, come back to normal. Move, even blink, or swallow, and he'll go where he is going, the full distance.

'And take that bloody thing out of her mouth! I'm sick of seeing it dangling there, she looks like a fucking dog!'

With his eyes front, still fixed on the road, Mick grabs the bottle from Frances's mouth so roughly that the teat she is sucking on tears, and she immediately starts crying, shocked, high-pitched screams.

So it is me who explodes.

'Get off her, GET OFF HER, you stupid bastard! What's the matter with you, you've hurt her.'

And I'm right, looking at Frances's mouth, her bottom lip has turned bright red, blood appearing in an instant. I can't make sense of this, how could her mouth be bleeding from Mick simply tugging a bottle away from her? He must have scratched her, caught her with his ring. I can't seem to think straight, the sight of Frances crying and shocked by the taste of blood bursts up in me like a dam, and there is rushing in my ears.

'Stop the car! Stop the car you fucking git, I need to look at Frances!'

But I'm not looking at Frances, I'm looking at Mick, and trying to reach across her to get at him, scratching the side of his face with my hands, yelling 'See how you like it, do you like it? Do you?'

He slams on the brakes and we are thrown forward, but the distance between our seat and the windscreen is much further than in a car, only Mick's head even touches the pane. A small clonking sound – his forehead on glass. He doesn't seem to notice this, to be aware of Frances screaming, he is opening his truck door, I know what is coming next but I'm fumbling in my bag for a tissue for Frances, my heart dancing and bumping but saying 'Ssssh, sssh, it's OK, only a little nip, it was an accident, Daddy didn't mean it, don't cry Frankie . . .' What is important is to reassure Frances. The way she is crying is horrible, she has started to shake, she is red all over, I am scared to see her so scared, my baby, it is terrible.

'Get out of the car, you bitch.'

Mick has opened the door on my side. I glance at his cheek, see the weird red scratches my nails have made; two of them have drawn blood. I don't have to look at his eyes to know their expression; the pupils dilated and filling the blue almost to black.

'Mick, Mick, I'm sorry, Frances is scared, think about Frances, I was mad about Frances, I'm sorry . . .'

His hand is around my upper arm, it feels as if a band of iron has encircled it; my arm flimsy and thin, a stick of macaroni. I'm turned away from him, trying to soothe Frances, dabbing at her mouth with the tissue, wanting the strange shaking to stop but it hasn't and that's all I can think about, I can scarcely even feel Mick dragging me from the truck.

'Come out here you fucking bitch and face me. Look at my face! Look what you've done!'

'Mick, Mick, don't hurt me.'

I've never said this before, I feel ashamed to say it like this, to stop fighting and to beg, but this time I'd better, this time is different, something has already snapped and with Frances so frightened I just want it to be over, I can't think of a way to get it over.

There is no time to duck and I don't see the fist which hits my nose, my mouth, catches me once on the shoulder, and then Mick is running, shouting as he runs up the gravel road, away from the truck. As the pain cracks over the bridge of my nose, my hands fly up to my face and I feel wet pouring from between my fingers and hands and I keep my eyes tight shut, trying with all my strength not to scream, a long, long howl, but I mustn't, I must get a towel, and think about Frances.

Tears stream from somewhere, I don't think I am crying, it's just an automatic response to the pain in my nose, tears mixing with the blood, and I stay for as long as I dare with my face in my hands, and then I throw my head back and wait for the bleeding to stop. I can hear smaller sobs from Frances, and standing beside the truck, slightly out of her line of vision, I say in a nasal wet voice: 'It's all right Frankie, don't cry, I'm here, just a minute . . .'

I know she saw what happened, but I don't want her to see my face all bloody and smeared. With my head back, blood running into the back of my throat, I reach in the truck for the towel I brought and put it up to my face. It smells of Frances's clean body, and the earthy smell of the river. Gingerly I bring my head back down and wince at the sight of the stained towel. When I feel sure that most of the blood has gone from around my upper lip and nose, I climb back into the truck, unstrap Frances and lift her onto my knee.

For the first time in a long while, she lets me cuddle her. Properly cuddle her, burying my face in the top of her head, feeling her snug little shape and the warmth from her seep into my chest, and for the first time ever, I want to absorb her back inside me; draw her in, under the skin, to the one time when I did everything right, the one place I could keep her safe.

'Frankie, it's all right. There, there, all right now, don't cry. Ssssh, I'm here, it's all right.'

The shaking in her little body has started up a shaking in mine. My nose, my sinuses, my forehead are all throbbing, I'm holding her tight but I wish I could put my hands over my ears, shut out the wails rising to the trees.

## 15

While Mick is sleeping, I watch him, straining my eyes in the half-light, holding my pillow. It is almost a full moon and in the blue light I see the tremble of his bottom lip as his breath flows over it.

I lift the pillow and place it lightly, light as a sheet of paper, over his face. He carries on sleeping. I wait, shivering, to see if he will move it or notice. Mick is deeply asleep. The pillow rises and falls softly. An owl gives a low hoot, soft as velvet and close to the cabin.

Inside, I am ticking. Tick tick tick. I shift myself as silently as possible until I am leaning over Mick, breathing heavily. And then, because I can't think how else to do it, I slowly lower my entire weight onto the pillow, hold the edges down with my elbows, use my body weight to force the pillow over his face. It takes all my energy to do this, to hold the pillow down and keep it there, and even through the feathers I can feel his features sticking up, the nose and chin bony and jagged, like knives, or nails. He is so deeply asleep that he can't wake up and make sense of what is happening; he twitches and flicks his legs in a half-hearted way, but instead of the struggle I had expected I feel the pillow sucked into his mouth, feel his chest beneath me caving in, until I am falling into it; my knee is in his throat, his chin is in my stomach, and as the air squeezes out of him, his sharp jaw suddenly softens and melts.

I wake up panting and sealed in sweat. Mick turns over onto one side and gives a snuffled cough. Something else woke me, not just the dream. Something outside. There's someone outside the cabin. On our wooden deck I hear a distinct thud thud. I listen again. Or is it tap tap? Could it be shoes, steps, or something else? What should I do, should I wake Mick – but I hate Mick, we aren't speaking, we're still skirting round each other, we don't know how to be after last week, how to carry on . . . Thud. A loud thud. What could it be? Coyotes again? The tread is too heavy for coyotes, the sound is more like a shoe or—

'Rita? Did you hear that?'

'You're awake! Yes, I'm listening. What do you think it is?'

The outline of Mick sits up, and I strain to see him more clearly, see his face. Is he smiling?

'Is the torch on your side? Or the candles? I'll have a look.'

I feel under my side of the bed and find the torch. When he switches it on an immense relief floods me, with the beam of light across the blanket. It's Mick being awake, coming to life.

He stands up and pads over to his trainers, shines the torch into the dirty grey sole and puts them on, without doing them up. He points the torch beam at the ground and I watch as various bits of the cabin appear and disappear; the oil-barrel stove; a carrier bag with used nappies in it; a can of Colman fuel.

Opening the door makes enough noise to frighten anything away. I'm sitting up in bed, I hear Mick whisper 'wow!' so I whisper 'What? What was it?'

'A deer,' he whispers back, 'right on the deck. It was the hooves we could hear.'

'Must have been chewing at the bits of kinnickkinnick I've been picking. I left them tied to the door so that Frances couldn't reach.'

The sound of Mick having a long pee and then coming in again, closing the door behind him, closing out some moonlight, but shining the torch again to find the bed.

The bed creaks as he sits down on it.

'Why are you drying kinnickkinnick anyway?' he asks.

'For you to smoke.'

'Why?'

'It's better for you than dope.'

'Oh.' A pause. 'Fancy a cup of tea?' he says.

Another long pause. Then, 'Yes, I do. I'll light the lamp.'

I'm shivering as I pump up the fuel in the lamp, pulling the little handle in and out, then hold a match to the pungent fuel, taking care not to touch the brittle white gauze.

Mick is filling the kettle from the water carrier and at the same time as he says, 'We need some more water tomorrow,' I say 'We must get some Colman fuel tomorrow.'

'You are staying then?' asks Mick, reaching for his packet of Top to roll a cigarette. His back is to me.

'What?'

'I thought you would go back to England. After what happened.'

My hand goes up to my nose, stroking the bridge, feeling for tenderness. I sit down in the chair nearest to the stove and pick up a Ponderosa twig we keep nearby to poke about in it, stirring up red embers from the grey.

'The squat's finished,' I say. 'Nicola says the council have put a steel door on it . . .'

I find a log near the oil barrel and place it in, gingerly opening the door with my fingernails and finding the metal is still hot to the touch. Mick turns around, his tongue sticking out, licking the paper before rolling it.

'I'm such a shit. I'm no good.'

'You're not a shit,' I tell him. 'Don't say that.'

'But look what I did to Frances. Look what I'm doing to

you. You're so frightened the whole time. You jump at the slightest thing.'

'I'm not – I don't.'

Mick shakes his head, sitting down opposite me. A new chair, Jim gave it to us, a chair that looks like it exploded, coughing up stuffing. The lamp is hanging just above him, hissing loudly, and a moth bats itself at it, making weird, enormous shadows just above Mick's head. I'm staring at these, hugging my knees up to my chest in my usual bedtime outfit; leggings, T-shirt and Mick's sweater. I fix my eyes on the bat-like shapes the moth is making.

'I still want things to work, Mick.' A long silence. 'I like it here.'

He finishes rolling the cigarette, says nothing.

'I've been thinking, 'I say, as the moth settles for a moment, three inches from Mick's head. 'Nancy has this friend, an arty one, who sells her paintings at these weekend Barter Fairs. She said she'd introduce us. Maybe her friend would know where I could get some gigs or teach music or something.'

He still doesn't speak, so I carry on.

'I mean, get a job. That's what I need. Maybe Nancy's friend knows how I can carry on with my therapy training – complete a counselling course in Sinkalip, or go over the border to BC and then maybe – I mean, there must be people who need therapy out here, too.'

Mick laughs sharply.

I poke at the log in the bottom of the barrel stove until the charcoal underbelly starts to smoke, and finally a sliver of blue flame appears.

'You could change, Mick. I mean, I got pregnant so soon – before we had a chance—'

The kettle interrupts with a quick screech, and Mick leaps up to stifle it. We both look at Frances, a lump under the mosquito net. But she doesn't wake up.

Mick pours water into our mugs, holding a tea-towel over

the handle of the kettle. His unlit cigarette is balanced on the arm of his chair. When he hands me the mug I look at his face, the first time our eyes have met for a week. Then we both look away.

Mick stirs sugar into his tea, he concentrates on his spoon, fishes out the tea-bag and flops it inside the stove. Then he fixes his gaze on the flames licking around the log.

'It's not good for Frances, is it?' he says, his voice dull, his eyes fixed on the fire.

'No.'

'Oh God, Rita, I'm such a mess. You've got to help me. I wish you could help me.'

The outline of his face, his profile, seems to wobble, to actually tremble and reshape in front of my eyes. It must be the lamplight, but it seems to me that it is Mick, a peculiar quality of Mick's, this ability to go from hard to soft, to drift away and towards me like smoke. I take one sip of the hot tea, scald my tongue.

'Don't cry,' I say. My voice comes out quietly, a tiny voice, weightless. The log crackling and the lamp hissing and the moth flapping are all louder than my voice. These things have substance, my voice doesn't.

'Don't cry, Mick,' I try again. I love you. But this time even the wind blowing between the logs is louder than me, drowns the words, steals them before they're spoken.

## 16

We have a local map now from the drugstore in Sinkalip. I pin it to a log next to my side of the bed and wake to its green National Forest promises, with the tantalising Pasetan Wilderness at the furthest edge to the left, nearly obliterated by one of Frances's jammy fingerprints. I fancy a visit to Top Lake, which is a few miles higher up Mount Coyote.

Mick is busy putting an upstairs floor in the cabin; made from two by fours, some brought with us from Carole's, some bought in a constructor's back yard at Goldtown. For weeks now, I've been holding the ladder while he works on the burgeoning floor above me. The routine is this: I pass him the drill, he drills the hole, passes it back, then I pass him a nail from the nail bag, then his hammer, then the drill again; or else I'm running in and out switching the generator on and off, according to his instructions. Frances plays around us, copying Mick, shouting things like: 'Genny – on! Reeta, Genny – off!' and making bbbbrrrr noises while I struggle to pull the chord that starts it up. The generator was our big outlay. Now the dollars are really down, so after this Mick has to get work. Anyhow, the season is right. Apple-picking will start soon.

'I might take a walk to Top Lake,' I shout, over the noise of the generator, and Mick's drill, and Frances revving and brrrm-brrrmmming.

'What about Frankie?' Mick says, over his shoulder, laying the drill down and placing a nail in the hole he just made. The upstairs floor is supported by log beams, most of them were already in place, meaning that there was an upstairs here once. Mick reminds me of this whenever I voice doubts about falling through the floor.

'She'll be asleep soon,' I say. 'I'll put her down for her nap. I'll only be gone a couple of hours and it's so hot. She'll sleep for ages once she's off . . .'

He grunts his agreement and nods towards the next two by four, meaning for me to pass it up to him. I'm irritated that he always assumes Frances is my responsibility. Couldn't he offer to look after her for once while I do a bit of exploring?

Anyhow, I need a bath. I'm sick of washing in a bowl of cold water and my hair is so greasy that it's more brown than blonde these days. I gather together my things and settle Frances into her cot with Sindy and Raccoon and a weird doll that I found under the deck which is bendy and has hair matted with soil, but which Frances loves. I fill her bottle with water and leave it beside the cot for her when she wakes up. She stares at me, her cheeks flushed, too tired to put up a fight, although she usually resists a lunchtime nap, preferring to be grouchy for the next eight hours until bedtime. Sensing that I've won, that her glazed stare is actually an effort to force her eyes open, I arrange the mosquito net over her, and put the rest of the bug repellent in my bag for me.

'Good girl, Frances. Little nap. I'll be back soon.'

'See you later,' Mick says, watching me pull a vest and shorts on over my bikini, and put my glasses back on. Stepping out into the bright midday light, hearing him whistling as he sweeps up the pale shavings from the drill, I feel like I'm escaping, skiving off school.

I'm surrounded by chatter; the birdsong out here is incredible, I notice it more each day. Because it's otherwise so silent, tiny sounds are magnified and I find myself properly listening to them. There must have been birds in London. There were birds in London of course. Pigeons in the loft at the squat making a purring noise that sometimes woke me in the early hours of the morning and convinced me that someone on the floor above was making love; soft, rhythmic sighings. But nothing like this blizzard of sound; whistles, fluting cries sweeping up and down a range of notes, calls and replies and angry chatterings. I've even learned to distinguish the ones I hear most; I've worked out why a chickadee is called a chickadee, which I suppose anybody with half a brain would know, and that a nuthatch makes a kind of nasal 'yank yank' sound.

I kick pines down the drive, reach the road without looking back to the cabin. I've left the map pinned to the log; I've always liked getting lost.

It's quite a hike and uphill too. Hot and dusty, the big stones of the gravel road poke through my trainers as I whistle, dawdle, pat various trees as I pass them, keep my eyes peeled for vanilla leaf, which I can dry out, use to scent the clean washing. The roads are lined with fireweed, Indian paintbrush and occasionally a flower, deep purple and succulent which I don't know the name of. Might be Western Monkshood, the purple is intense enough, the petals are plump enough. Yes, probably Monkshood. Wish I'd brought my notebook.

A blue pick-up passes me. It hoots and the guy inside it waves, for reasons unknown to me. Maybe because I'm the only person walking on Mount Coyote on a Tuesday (Wednesday?) in late July. Maybe for the same reason men used to honk their horns at me when I was fourteen when me and my friend Jackie played on Rainham Marshes in our cap-sleeved T-shirts and A-line denim skirts, and every passing vehicle in summer seemed to be full of hollering men with their shirt-sleeves rolled up.

I feel fourteen again right now. Maybe it's the shorts – the freckly legs sticking out, covered in scabs from the deer-brush and the long scratchy grasses around the cabin. These are not the waxed, tanned legs of a grown woman of twenty-six. These are the kind of legs Frances will have one day. Hairy, smeared with dirt. Protruding ankle bones, filthy trainers. I have a sudden complete image of Frances at fourteen, her blonde hair darker, smoothed into an attempt at a bob, Mick's blue eyes, my freckles, my pointy chin, my tough little legs, my top-heavy figure, the bane of my life at fourteen; the mouth – downturned, accusing – all her own.

I stand still for a moment. Frances as a teenager – as real as a photograph, a memory. It's like time got switched around, the future's somewhere I've already been to and already feel the loss of. Maybe all Mums do this, I tell myself. Don't worry about Frances. She's sleeping. What has she got to accuse me of? I'm not the one who made her lip bleed. But that's sheer bravado; I ache with guilt whenever I picture Frances in the truck with her little wet mouth trembling, the splash of bright red on the bottom lip, her big eyes asking me to do the impossible: make the pain stop and send the scary Daddy away.

*They never remember*. That's what my Mum says. 'It's amazing how children bounce back, you know; all those childhood scrapes and knocks, but they never remember them. It's you who never bloody forgets the time you rushed into casualty with a screaming three-year-old who just fell out of a tree.'

She's talking about one of my brothers, Dan I think, she told me that story often but the brothers always merge into one; one big anxiety, one big headache. In memories, my brothers muddle together like the mass of dirty socks that used to get thrown on the kitchen floor on wash day, Saturday mornings. Mum standing over the twin-tub dragging out the soaking football socks, muttering to herself: 'whose are these?' It was years before she got an automatic, then I missed the smell of the hot wooden tongs mixed with

Persil. My job to pop the rubber hose over the sink when it started to spin; 'Thank God for you Rita,' Mum says, 'thank God I finally got a girl.'

But I don't agree with her – I wish I did. Children do remember and they never forgive. I remember more than she thinks I do.

Top Lake is further than I anticipated but worth the effort. The straggly forest of trees on either side of the road opens at last to a small clearing, revealing the flattened-grass path down to the lake, surrounded by forest. A sign on a tree announces Okanogan National Park and a handwritten one beneath it, 'No Hunting'.

The lake has a deep green centre, the edges are swampland full of dead bulrushes and yellow waterlilies on huge lily pads. I've never seen giant lily pads before. The kind that Jeremy Fisher sits on in Frances's story book. Movements in the water, tiny splashes catch my eye and I watch a small bird hop from pad to pad. I set my bag down, spread the towel out on the grass path.

In the centre of the lake is a stand of dead pines, an eerie circle of grey. Top Lake is surrounded by climbing banks of trees, I feel as if I'm at the bottom not the top of the mountain, the lake dropped like a shiny pebble in a dark, dark green forest, reaching up to the skies.

I take my T-shirt off and strip down to my bikini. The smell of my own sweat is strong, mixed with the bug repellent, an overpowering sticky lavender. Mosquitoes, violet-tails, the biting black fly and an assortment of other buzzing horrors seem suddenly to surround me, so I'm wondering if the bug repellent will really do the trick out here. These things get worse near water.

I run hands through my sweaty hair, over my dirty face. I take off my trainers. I place my glasses carefully on top of my shorts so that I can see them easily when I come out of the water.

A few feet away from the spot I've chosen there are signs of a fire, a few charred logs, a black spot on the grass, an empty Dr Pepper can. Also a litter of these weird little brass things, the size of Frances's thumb; hollow cases with a cap on one end. I pick one up, without my glasses I have to bring it right up to my face to see it. Vaguely I know these little pellets have something to do with a gun but I'm not sure what they're called. Mick would know.

I walk barefoot on the rough grass to the swampy part of the lake. If it weren't for the litter and the can I could believe I was the only person who'd ever been here, and I like that feeling, I resent the intrusion.

I stretch up to the sun before I step into the water; a big stretch, me and the trees pointing up to the blue, blue sky. A raven flies over and the water, creeping up to my shins and knees and now thighs is icy, clutching like fingers on goose-pimpled flesh.

At first I don't like it, I have to wade through the lilies, the long thick stems brush my legs under the water, my feet touch soft soil which seems to dissolve beneath my soles. It's an effort of will not to really feel these things; otherwise I might feel sick, turn back. The water is now at waist height, and the huge lily pads each with a fat clump of bunched yellow flower, a scrunch of yellow tissues, at elbow height, perfect for resting on. I have to push myself through this part, this is the hard part, the yukky bit where half of me is warm and dry, half cold and wet, claimed by clasping roots.

I knew when I woke up this morning that I was desperate to swim. I've walked all this way in midday 100 degree heat because ever since I saw Top Lake on the map I longed to be here.

I have to fight my distaste, head for the green centre of the water because I know I will feel better there. When I can't touch the ground any longer, when the lily roots can't grab me, touch me, where I can't feel anything except cold cold water and floating and clean, this is what heaven must feel like, heaven or death or one of those things; floating, being held. I turn over on my back, close my eyes, feel my hair spread out around me in a fine icy net. The sun pours down on me, melts my body like an ice lolly, turning my yellow limbs liquid, melting me into the lake.

## 17

Coming out from Top Lake, there is a man, sitting on the grass, watching me.

I'm wading through the lily roots, my heart thumping from the swim, skin singing. I have to keep walking but with him there I'm intensely aware of myself suddenly from the outside; a small blonde with big tits stretched into a too small wet bikini. I resist the urge to crouch back down in the water but surreptitiously pull the bikini bottoms up and smooth the material properly over my buttocks. A movement I've seen a thousand times; women emerging from swimming pools, one hand on their knicker line trying to subtly rearrange it. Fuck him. Five minutes ago I was as unselfconscious as a nine-year-old.

'Hi,' he says.

He's sitting right next to my towel. I have to step up to him, dripping and breathing heavily. He is smoking. I stare down at his boots, their broken tips, the ankles of his tatty jeans, and the thick lumber jacket he is sitting on, the navy-blue lining torn and dirty. He has a belt with a huge silver buckle and some letters on it, a black T-shirt where the neck has stretched from too many washes. Short brown hair and a thin face. Probably late twenties. Younger than Mick. No features. Where are my glasses?

'You looking for these? Didn't want to sit on them.'

He hands me the glasses and I put them on. The face comes into view with its regular features, the slightly sharp jaw-line; green eyes, squinting in the sun, fine creases at the corners of his eyes and around the mouth, tanned skin. Straight nose.

'Thanks,' I say, shaking the grasses off my towel before I wrap myself in it, taking care to shake it away from him. 'Am I in your spot or something?'

The camp fire, the gun cartridges, must be his. The way he's sitting, with his knees up, like he intends to spend all day here.

He doesn't bother to answer, takes another drag on the cigarette, stubs it into the earth.

'Where you from? Australia?'

'England. London.'

'Ah. You're the English couple, right? Living in Pike's old place.'

I smile. Amazing how empty Mount Coyote feels yet is just like a village for gossip. I feel better now I have the towel around me but there is the problem of how to get dressed. And washing myself in the lake is out of the question, now. Still, I feel clean after my swim. I secure the towel under my arms and sit down next to him, rummage in my bag for my brush.

'You on holiday?' he asks, his eyes on the lake.

'No. We bought it. Pike's place, as you call it. The cabin and seven acres of land. Mick – my boyfriend – wants to do it up. Maybe build another cabin on the property after a while.'

He nods, seems incurious. I struggle with my wet hair and the brush while he reaches in his back pocket for a squashed packet of cigarettes, matches with 'The Round-Up Café' on them.

'We went there. The café in Sinkalip,' I say, nodding to the matches.

He grins. 'What d'you think? Good coffee, lousy hamburgers. I work there. In the kitchen. Sometimes.'

I'm trying to decide if I feel OK, sitting in my bikini next to a strange man, miles from nowhere. But I do. It's something to do with the bright sun-light, bouncing off every blade of grass, highlighting every ant, warming my bare legs and arms, the still lake which has closed up now as if nothing ever entered it. Broad daylight.

He gestures with the cigarette packet, offers his last cigarette. Virginia Slims. Shouldn't he be smoking Marlboro? I shake my head.

'Don't smoke? Sensible. You're fit, huh. A great swimmer. You know that?'

I beam at the compliment.

'My big brother taught me. Dan. The eldest. I used to swim in races and things when I was a kid and I did all my life-saving awards, bronze, silver, gold, you know? I don't know if you have them here . . .?'

He nods. 'Yeah, something like that. Don't swim much myself. Don't like the snakes.'

'What?'

'Garter snakes. Harmless enough but I can't stand them.'

He suddenly laughs.

'Your face. Didn't you see any snakes? C'mon, I'll show you.'

He gets up, strides over to the water's edge and I follow. We both stare into the bulrushes and reeds and lily pads until he says 'There!' and points. A stripe of yellow and black as something on the grassy bank disappears into the swampy water at the edge of the lake.

I push my glasses onto my nose. 'There's another,' I say, but the one I spot is dead, its mouth stretched over a piece of dead fish, like a stocking half-pulled onto a foot.

He kicks it with his boot, rolls it over.

'Bit off more than he could chew, I guess.'

He kicks it back into the water. Studies my face. 'They're harmless,' he assures me.

'Don't you have snakes in England?' he asks when we sit back down. Him on his coat, me on my stretched out towel. I'm practically dry and – so what? He's OK. Broad daylight.

'Only grass snakes but I can't remember ever seeing one. I mean – I grew up in London and Essex. I've seen snakes in the zoo. I think there is supposed to be one poisonous snake in England but I can't remember. Probably extinct by now anyway.'

'Not hot on that stuff, huh? Native wildlife?' He is teasing, I think, maybe an English accent always sounds like a school teacher to an American.

'There isn't much, in England. I mean, not like here ...' I shrug, shy of how gushing I feel, how much I want to tell him about loving Top Lake, loving the mountain.

There is a silence, punctured by the angry chirping protest chipmunks make when their nest is threatened. He tenses; something about him, despite the relaxed way he's sitting, is alert, waiting.

'What are you doing here?' I ask. It sounds rude, but I'm curious, and there's no other way to ask.

He drags his attention back from the trees to give me a big grin.

'What's your name?'

'Rita.'

'Well, Rita. What I'm rightly doing here is nobody's business but mine.'

He is smiling, he's playful, stretching out one long leg in the pointy-toed boots to dig a track in the soft-grass with the heel. He takes the last draw from the cigarette, rests his eyes on my belly for a second then glances away.

'You a Government agent or something? A cop?'

I shrug, knowing he doesn't need an answer.

Finally he cracks up laughing, stands up.

'Well what do you think I'm doing, Rita from England?'

He wanders over to where the forest begins again, to the trees and to the sign saying No Hunting. With a small movement he reaches down and produces a long thin khaki bag. Puts his hand inside it and draws out a rifle.

He carries it back to where I'm sitting. Lays it beside himself and sits back down.

'I'm poaching. You're swimming in my spot – or I'm poaching in yours. Most times I'm the only one here.'

'What do you poach?' I ask.

'Oh, you know. Grouse, quail, birds, deer . . .'

'Oh no! Deer. How can you shoot a deer? They're so lovely, aren't they protected or something . . .?'

'Not in Hunting Season. Problem is Hunting Season is two months off. And I don't have a licence. White tails. Good eating. You should try it sometime.'

'I couldn't. I was offered some recently – we went for this meal at Jim and Nancy's. Do you know them, they live a mile or so down the mountain from us?'

'Sure I know them. You were offered deer? A doe? Was it good?'

He seems to know about this. He's smiling, at the same time fidgeting, feeling in all his pockets, the pocket of his jacket, gets up to feel in the khaki bag he's left in the trees. He comes back with another packet of Virginia Slims.

'I couldn't eat it,' I say. 'I don't know why. Maybe because Nancy said it had been caught with a young one. It was a mother. I can't explain. I felt sick.'

'They're easy to catch then. They run, but they always pause to look back. Looking for the young. That's when you shoot.'

He cups his hands to his mouth as he lights up, visibly relaxes after the first inhalation. He's looking at me, he's not grinning now.

'I got fired from my job at the Round-Up. So I'm just catching myself some food.'

All the while he is talking I can see his eyes are quick, watching the trees, the bulrushes at the edge of the lake, then glancing up at the sky as a huge raven flies over with a scream.

'I once shot one of a pair of ravens on my property. Big mistake. The mate wouldn't leave me alone. She came back night after night, squawking and bleating.'

'Did you shoot her too?'

He laughs. 'You think I'm about to say yes, don't you? Didn't have the heart.'

A plop in the lake as a fish jumps. Our eyes fix on the spot.

'You against fishing too?'

'Yes. But only cos it's diabolically boring.'

He laughs.

'There's violence in everything. It's natural.'

'I know that but—'

'You ever seen an owl light on a chipmunk? Or a bob-cat sink its teeth into a snow-shoe hare in winter? That's a hell of a mess. Blood and snow and fur all mixed up – they leave a cache, you know, to come back to later. Or wolves. They piss on theirs so no one else will touch it. Raw meat stinking of wolf piss. That's what nature is.'

'That's corny, people are always saying that. How cruel nature is. Wolves make good fathers.'

'What?'

'We went to this place. A ranch with wolves on it, saved from people who were keeping them as pets. Wolf Haven. The guide told us. In wolf families the male plays the major part in nurturing, in raising the young.'

He smiles. 'That right?' is all he says. After a moment's thought he concedes, 'Guess it can be used to justify anything. Either way. Nature. Calling something natural.'

I'm pleased. I have a tiny sensation of triumph, of having

been reassured, without knowing that I was requiring reassurance. A delicious feeling of relaxation is creeping up my body, after my swim. I like him, I decide.

'You don't have a gun at your cabin? Your old man got one?' he asks.

'No, of course not. What do we need a gun for?'

'You must be the only two up here without one. What d'you do if you have a prowler, or a rattle snake, a bear in winter?'

'Send Mick out. He'd scare anything off.'

'Your old man a Mike Tyson lookalike?'

'No, not really. I mean, he's not black, for a start . . .' I hesitate, wondering how seriously he meant his last comment, wondering where this longing has come from, this overwhelming desire to confide in someone about Mick.

A cloud dampens the sun for a second, my high spirits nose dive. It's getting late. Surely I've been gone ages. Mick is such a long, long story.

'I don't suppose you know what time it is?' I ask, after a pause.

His eyes hold mine for a moment, then he glances at his watch.

'Twenty after five. Name's Ryan by the way. How do you do . . .'

He holds out his hand, the one without the cigarette. He smiles, and I smile back at a tiny shadowy version of myself reflected in his pupils.

'I have to go. I said I wouldn't be long.'

I stand up, forget to be embarrassed and pull the shorts and vest on over my bikini. My fingers feel cool on my hot stomach and the metal buttons on the cut-off Levi shorts burn to the touch. I crouch down to do up my trainers.

'I have a little girl. She'll be missing me,' I say, a deliberate remark, an attempt to defend myself. I've got a child, I'm a mother, I'm happy. You can't tempt me. Don't tempt me.

'See you around, Rita. Now I can get back to blowing the brains outa them Bambis . . .'

'See you. Nice talking to you.'

Too English. Too formal. But there isn't a useful, comfortable phrase for what I really want to say. Thank you. For what? For listening to me? But I didn't say anything, nothing important.

I am aware of him behind me, still sitting with his legs stretched out, smoking, facing the lake as I stride down towards Dry Gulch Road, one hand on the strap of my shoulder bag, the other flapping at mosquitoes. Funny how I didn't notice them for the last few hours. Now my arms and legs are pink with bites and the damn things are back with a vengeance.

I tell Mick about the giant lilies and the circle of dead pines in the middle of Top Lake and about the yellow and black garter snakes. He says he remembers snakes like that from when he was a kid. Maybe you shouldn't swim in Top Lake, he scolds because what about leeches and look at you now you're covered in mosquito bites. He looks at me with an odd little frown darkening his blue eyes and then helps me blob calamine lotion on the bites until I look like a weird mottled creature all pink and white and then he starts kissing me and I say God you fancy anything but I'm warm and sleepy from my swim and the little taps from the cold calamine-soaked cotton wool in Mick's rough fingers set up a rhythm. I put my hand over his and start tapping some more in places without bites, lift up my T-shirt and tap lotion all over myself, laughing.

'I've got bites on my thighs too, look,' I offer, rolling up my shorts, and then turning round and rolling them up at the back, showing him places where he dutifully dabs further, all the time kissing me, his mouth at my neck; that way Mick has of descending on me in a sudden attack of kisses and murmurs, oblivious to everything else.

Frances is playing on the deck, breaking up bits of bread and squashing ants with them and she doesn't notice when Mick and I go upstairs.

We now have an upstairs. Mick has heaved the bed up there. Tomorrow he'll put the rest of the floorboards in, nailing them to the beams. There's no way we could get the bed up there once that's finished; there is only a flimsy log ladder and a gap a couple of feet square.

Frances holds the bottom of the log ladder and whines, wanting to come upstairs, but unable to get past the bottom rung, or more importantly, to see past it.

I hear her but the sun is pouring in through the window nearest the bed as Mick steers me onto it, onto the muddle of unmade sheets. My body is hot and tired and the tingling stings from the bites are delicious, combining with Mick's chafed hands to bring my skin up to boiling point. I lie on the bed, flat-out, covered in the pasty calamine blobs and Mick throws himself at me with his usual haste; tearing off shorts and T-shirts.

There is only the sound of the two by fours squeaking and Mick taking short breaths, little sobs, in between the flurry of kisses, which are still descending, in my hair, in my neck, on my eyelids, on my breasts, and his body becomes red hot and slippery with sweat while I lie there in a blissful, knackered state letting him do all the work. Mick laughs at his 'lazy Rita' and rolls me over until I'm on top of him. The smell of the lake rises from my skin and with it an image, a faint image, which I push to the back of my mind. It's like swimming again, fast and heady, it's exactly the same, I can close my eyes and not think at all, give myself up to my sizzling body, spiralling up through the chimney pipe into the blue sky above.

Top Lake is wonderful and all mine. I plan to go there again, perhaps take Frankie for a bath one day. Maybe while Mick is working in the apple valley.

When we've dressed and pacified Frances with some nails and Mick's nail-bag to mess around with, I cook us a chilli with tinned kidney beans and tinned tomatoes and some giant red and green peppers and rice. The rice burns at the bottom because I misjudge how many logs in the fire and make it too hot so that the pan boils dry. We've run out of water to top the pan up with – we need another trip to Box Spring. Also, without water and with too many logs in the stove I don't know how to get the heat down.

But it all tastes fine with plenty of beer to wash it down.

'You gettin' mighty domesticated, Maam . . .' Mick drawls at me, plopping his packet of Top tobacco on his knee and rolling himself a cigarette, grinning at me in a fat, contented kind of way. When the cigarette is rolled he lifts Frances up onto his knee and the two of them sit there in a warm, stuffed-to-the-brim stupor, and I stare out of the open cabin door watching the chipmunks on the deck. Two small ones (I think the family is growing) run to the doorway, pause with their hands and noses twitching, fix their black beady eyes carefully on me and snatch at a piece of chopped pepper then whirl around, whisking the deck with their tails.

'It feels like a billion miles from Dalston. We couldn't be further if we were on the moon, could we?' I say, sleepily.

Mick blows a smoke ring out towards the cabin door. Slender shadows from the trees fall onto the deck. It's about eight o'clock, a breeze scatters cones and twigs and makes the shimmering blue-green of the Ponderosa tops sway.

'Don't think about it. I never think about it.'

'Don't you miss anyone? Spider? Or anything? Going to see Spurs play?'

'I hardly got there, last season. Probably only one game. No, don't miss anything in England. I miss my brother though. I miss Cherie-Rose.'

'What?'

It's like he just took a long sharp stick and poked me under the ribcage. I can't believe he said that. My heart leaps up under my chin and is thumping there while I wait to compose myself, to take a breath before asking, so that it comes out properly, not this frantic squeak inside me.

'Who was Cherie-Rose? You said it was no one important.'

Frances is snuggled with her head against Mick's bare chest. His hand rests on her blonde head, one finger gently stroking as he narrows his eyes, inhaling.

'She was my Mum. Died when I was ten.'

I can see a semi-circle of bright water at his lower lashes, under the deep blue eyes, but it doesn't spill over.

'Mick.' It comes out softly, in a voice with a crack. 'I – you said – I thought it was a girlfriend. I thought your Mum's name was Rose. Your brother speaks of her as Rose. That's why we called Frankie Frances Rose. That's what you said.'

'Rose, Cherie-Rose, what's the difference?'

'None, I suppose. It's just – your tattoo – all this time – I don't know. You never tell me anything.'

'Always trying to puzzle me out.' His tone is a statement, without reproof, his voice barely a murmur.

A fresh scattering of twigs and pine cones lands on the deck and this time the wind running through the treetops is stronger, pulls them with an invisible string, so that they all bend together.

'A storm's coming.' Mick gently places Frances on her bum on the rug in front of his chair and stands up to look for the radio. He messes around with it, trying to tune into Wenatchee Station for the weather news, but all day it's been a pledge drive. 'For only five dollars a month you can contribute to this great public service, this wonderful public radio ... Be informed, be aware, be involved ...' After listening to this for a few seconds Mick gives up.

'Better get the logs in,' I venture, as another gust of wind slams the cabin door shut. The chipmunks have disappeared. There is no bird song.

Frances jumps up, eyes sparkling, picking up on the change of atmosphere.

'Daddy, Daddy, Daddy . . .' she crows, following Mick around. We run outside, filling our arms with the chopped logs and piling them haphazardly beside the barrel-stove. Frances gets under Mick's feet as he rushes to close the windows on the truck, carries in the generator, the chainsaw, and I whizz around picking up toys, and dragging the washing from its line between the trees. Already some of it has blown off and caught on the bushes and I get scratched untangling Mick's long football socks from the prickles on the Nootka rose and chokecherry.

Loud scatterings on the roof as a hail of cones and sticks land there. The first clap of thunder is not a roll from an English storm, but like gun-shot.

'Wow. An electric storm!' Mick says, excitedly. He picks up Frances and twirls her around, and then hugs her as another boom of thunder makes her jump out of her skin.

Suddenly the cabin is lit up with purple light – like ultra violet.

'My God, Rita, did you see that?'

Mick is delighted, stands near the window with Frances in his arms, staring out at the trees. She is wide-eyed but entrusts herself to Mick, puts one fat hand up to his nose, touches his silver nose-stud, then his stubbly chin and follows his gaze.

The trees bend in a long dark dance together and the rain cracks down in sheets. It's cold now, my teeth are chattering. I stand next to the two of them and Mick stretches out his arm around my waist. In between the lightning it's pretty dark although the sun is setting behind the trees. The only way we know this is that the next flash of lightning is pink, and there are suddenly treetops as far as the eye can see, silver and spiderwebby. I can hear ominous dripping and thudding upstairs and sizzling on top of the barrel-stove as rain lands on the hot surface, and hisses in the metal chimney.

'Mick – I hate to say this, but . . .'

Another pinky-purple flash of lightning, as clear as daylight. Mick's face illuminated in rose-pink light, bright and excited is frightening to me, there is something giddy about him, the pupils are dilated and I know him well enough by now to know. I mustn't mention Cherie-Rose again. Not at the moment, much as I want to.

'The upstairs! The fucking roof! Is it coming in?'

He puts Frances down and dives for the ladder. A long groan from Mick confirms the worst. He starts barking out orders.

'Rita! Pass me up the bucket, all the pans and containers you can find . . . is that bit of tarpaulin down there or did we leave it outside?'

I gather the tarpaulin and climbing half way up the ladder, haul it up to him. He covers the bed with it, positions buckets, pans, cups, bowls, Frances's toy bucket, the washing-up bowl still full of dirty plates, all around the room. Now some water is dripping straight through the boards to the downstairs and the cabin floor has several darkening patches and a cacophony of drips and in some places, a steady thin stream of water.

'Oh no . . .' Mick is groaning, and Frances saying 'wet, wet' is running round, putting her hand out and catching drips.

I feel, as ever, useless, and scared. Wind is gusting through the cabin, swishing under the rug and scattering newspapers. The trees are cracking and moaning and I really daren't ask Mick, right at the moment, whether he thinks we're safe here. All those stories I read as a child, those dire warnings about not sheltering under trees, in case you get hit by lightning and here we are encircled by trees – just us three up here with no phone, no electricity, no nothing as far as I can see. But I mustn't let Mick, or especially Frances, know that I'm scared.

He comes down the ladder with wet shining in his fair hair, his mood defeated and miserable.

'Don't worry, we can fix the roof tomorrow,' I say. 'This won't last. A summer storm, it'll be dry by tomorrow. I've had a good idea. Surely this rain water is safe to drink? It's the same water in the well isn't it?'

'Yeah.'

'Well I'll collect some in the kettle outside. Then at least we'll have some water to boil up and make some tea.'

'The great British solution. Fucking tea. You can tell you're a bloody Brit, Rita, through and through.'

I decide not to take the bait. Let him be rude to me if he likes. He has so much invested in the cabin, in the life here, in making it work. Everything that goes wrong scares him, threatens his dream, threatens to spiral him back to Dalston, to the dole, or to Clapton bus garage, to diesel and dirt and high grey ceilings, peppered with pigeons.

I run outside with the kettle. Outdoors smells of wet pine and wet wood and the damp smoke from our fire. Rain soaks me in seconds. Back inside Frances is crying, standing at the bottom of the ladder calling up to Daddy.

I can hear Mick cursing upstairs as I come back inside, and a splash and a rattle as he kicks a can of water over.

Whether by accident or in temper I wouldn't like to guess.

Upstairs the containers are all full and some are already spilling over. The tarpaulin has small wet puddles on it. Mick is sitting on the bed, seemingly unaware that his weight is making the water run towards him, soaking the leg of his jeans.

'D'you want to pass some down to me and I'll empty them outside and pass them back up?' I ask, from the second rung of the ladder.

'What's the use?'

'Well – we have to sleep here tonight, don't we . . . might as well make some effort to keep out the rain.'

Mick stares up at the logs above him. It is easy to see where the rain is pouring in; there are huge gaps in the plastic covering the roof; places where the wind whips a torn piece of plastic, peeling it back like a shred of skin, exposing a wound.

'Why didn't I do the fucking roof first? Jeez, this could go on for days.'

'It won't. Surely it won't . . . it's summer.'

A cold drip lands right on my nose and I remember that I have come upstairs to get Frances a jumper, stuffed in the rucksack under the bed. After some rummaging – Mick doesn't help me at all, and his legs over the edge of the bed make it hard to drag the rucksack out – I find her Aran sweater and take it downstairs to Frances, who then doesn't want it on and flaps and slaps at me with a bony Sindy as I try to get it over her head.

'Frankie, it's cold and it's wet in here. You need a jumper on,' I insist, exasperated. Nothing I do is ever right.

'Daddy,' whines Frances.

The thunder is no longer overhead. I count between the lightning and the thunder . . . one, two, three, four seconds. Isn't that how far away it's supposed to be? Dan taught me that. If it's true then the storm is definitely retreating.

'I think it's easing off,' I call upstairs to Mick. There is no answer.

I fetch the kettle from outside and stick the lid back on and set it on the stove to boil, pushing a few more logs in the barrel to stoke up the fire. Seven seconds now between the lightning and the thunder. The drips are intermittent, instead of steady. The wind has died down.

I take a cup of tea up to Mick and find him sitting on the tarpaulin on the bed in exactly the same position, except that now he is sitting in a puddle of water. I hand him the mug and the towel I used at Top Lake, which reeks of bug repellent but at least is dry.

He rubs it on his hair, hugs the tea, stares off into space.

'Mick, what is it? Don't worry . . . We'll buy some roofing material – whatever we need, when you start working, and I'll help you with it, I promise. It'll probably stay dry 'til then. Or maybe Jim can help us, we could ask him. Perhaps we can afford that aluminium roofing like he has on part of his cabin – surely that's better . . .'

Mick stares into the scattered containers. A spider floats on the surface of the water inside a tupperware box.

'It's all a load of crap, isn't it?'

'What, what is?'

I sound panicky, I know. Drip drip on the roof. The rain has practically stopped.

'This. You, me. What's the point of any of it? It's all going to fall apart, like everything I do.'

'No, no it isn't Mick. I don't understand you – I don't know why you're so defeated by a thunderstorm.'

I try cuddling him, place my arms around his shoulders, pat his back, but it's like hugging a wet car tyre.

'Mick, maybe we could invite your brother up for a visit, one weekend? I mean he and Carole would make the trip from Mount Vernon wouldn't they – it'd be fun for them . . .'

He sips his tea. I hear Frances downstairs saying 'mipmunk' and her little footsteps as she chases one. Outside it is now spectacularly quiet.

'Perhaps even your Dad would come for a visit. I mean, I know you don't get on with him, but—'

Mick looks at me over his mug and seems to see me at long last. With forced brightness he says: 'OK, Rita. You don't have to go that far. Jon and Carole, fine. My Dad? No thank you.'

His tone is one of surrender. I don't understand, I know something about Mick without being able to say what it is, and I know that he knows I know it. It swims in the room between us, from one to the other. Despair floods from him, threatens to swamp me, carry me away.

'You're drenched,' I say and he stands up slowly, starts pulling the jeans off, rubs at his thigh with the towel.

*Don't be sad.*

*I love you, Mick.*

## 19

Something is brewing. Mick is brewing. The days feel hot and stiff and crackly, like balled up pieces of paper. Something bad is coming.

Two things go wrong; number one, we got the timing out for apple-picking, townies that we are. Whenever we drive into Goldtown the trees look fit to burst, but Jim says it will be another month at least before they need any pickers. So our money has practically run out and we have to write to Jon in Mount Vernon and ask him to mail us a money order for 200 dollars.

Number two: in the post office in Goldtown, picking up the money order, someone in the queue is staring at me.

'Hi, Rita.'

He is wearing a cap pulled down low and at first I wonder who is this American kid and how does he know my name? Then he says 'Been swimmin' lately?' and I see that he's not a tall kid but a grown man. Ryan.

I mutter something stupid and muddled and blush, and I know that Mick notices.

Mick doesn't comment until I've calmed down, until I think I'm safe. We've queued in the bank, cashed the money and are in King's Supermart. I'm pushing a huge trolley down the aisles with Frances squashed into the trolley seat, bouncing a box of CrackerJack on her knee.

'Who was that then?'

'Who?'

Reaching for a carton of chocolate milk. Not catching his eyes.

'The fucking hillbilly. Who's the fucking hillbilly?'

'His name's Ryan. He's a friend of Jim and Nancy's. Milwaukee or Budweiser?'

'I don't give a toss. Where d'you meet him?'

'At the lake. What are you getting all funny about? It was nothing, I only spoke two words to him—'

'You didn't tell me. You never said anything. No wonder you came back so fucking horny.'

'Mick.'

'I know you, Rita. You forget. I know you.'

'Milwaukee then. I'll get twelve. And a bottle of this Californian wine, too. What d'you think – it's pretty cheap.'

I'm tense, but determined. There's a man in one of the aisles in his King's Supermart overall, stacking bottles of cranberry juice. I see him looking at me, notice his eyes land on my chest like flies and just to push my luck completely, turn to Mick.

'Look, Mick – he's looking at me. Quick, aren't you going to thump him?'

A smile flits across Mick's face, but a bitter one, a forced one.

'OK, OK, so men look at you. But you don't have to stir quite so much, you know.'

After King's it's Leo's warehouse to price roofing. Mick isn't finished yet.

'What did you talk about?'

'Huh?'

'You and the Hillbilly. Ryan.'

'Oh, not much. Swimming. Poaching. He was poaching . . .'

'Bloody redneck. National Rifle Association. Fucking American fascists.'

'What d'you mean?'

'That bloody enormous belt buckle – NRA. You couldn't miss it. Or maybe he didn't have his trousers on when you met him?'

'Mick, for God's sake!' This comes out too vehemently. The belt buckle. Yes. I did notice it.

At least Leo's is a big place, and over here, by the cans of Colman fuel and twenty candles for a dollar and the giant water containers, there's no one to hear him. I'm still trying for a playful note, pretending I think he's joking.

After the warehouse we take a trip up to Old Holson, seven miles north of the cabin, on the Canadian border. There's a museum there about gold-mining, Mick fancies a look. And next to it is something I want to see – it's in the Coyote stories – the Wishing Stone.

We take the road north out of Goldtown past Black Diamond Lake, following the map, a proper road, not a dirt track. Small planes fly over and Mick says 'That's Canada there,' and I stare at the windscreen.

'What's up with you?' Mick says.

'Nothing. It's you who's in a bad mood . . .'

'No it fucking isn't.'

Squabbling. Childish. Squabbles in the car. Me and my brothers on long car journeys. Me and Billy were the worst. Once, he dropped Barbie's hairdryer out of the window and when I dug my nails into his arm and made him squawk in pain it was me that got the smack, Mum leaning over the back seat, randomly slapping at the legs and arms she could reach. 'She started it!' He always said that. The others would back him up. *She started it*.

Beside the road is open brushland, sage-brush and the occasional stand of Aspen, then open fields again with small patches of trees. Mick spots a Mule deer running in the distance – he says they get that name because of their ears, which are huge, like a donkey's – but she blends with the colours of the fields, I can't make out the ears. Frances is playing with a new toy from the supermart – a plastic red and yellow bag that Mick bought her with a picture of a cutesy girl on the front and the word 'Honey' in silver and gold. She unzips it, opens her mouth and dribbles into it. Then zips it up again.

'She likes her bag,' Mick says.

'Are you being sarcastic?'

'No, what d'you mean?'

'Nothing.'

The road is climbing and now we are on highlands, flat plains. By the roadside I spot the brightest yellow bird I've ever seen, I think I am mistaken and then I see another; fat-bellied, black-capped, it's gone in a splash of bright yellow. If Mick saw it he's given up trying to entrance me; this time he says nothing.

Old Holson looms up out of nowhere – a shabby huddle of wooden buildings and a tiny brick schoolhouse. Next to the schoolhouse is a log cabin – not much different from ours, only neater, and with the bark properly stripped – with a sign on it: Old Holson Museum.

There's no one to pay, no one around at all, in fact, so we drive right up to it and park the truck.

Mick and Frances go into the museum while I clean my glasses so I can read the information board at the doorway – a handwritten sign behind dusty, broken glass. The museum is the oldest log cabin in the area, built in 1912; Old Holson was a pioneer town, which boomed in the early twentieth century and was settled by prospectors and farmers; the cavalcade of history which has swept across Okanogan County in North Central Washington state has encompassed every element important to the Old West; bla bla bla.

Inside there is a stove made from an oil barrel, remarkably like the one Mick made, and a tiny wooden cot with a doll in it. On the farthest wall is a display of precious metals and gems which presumably was once behind glass. Now most of the metals are gone, instead only the curling cream-paper labels remain; Native Gold. Silver. Pyrite. Rose Quartz. Rose Quartz. *Cherie-Rose*. I take my glasses off and put them on the dashboard of the truck.

Mick is outside now, showing Frances some old pieces of rusty farm machinery which are lying around between the trees, making wild shadows on the grass. Horse-drawn plough, the sign says. Thresher. They all look the same to me. Everything looks the same – tired, broken and dangerous.

He is about to sit Frances on one of the pieces – a kind of huge plough – which looks lethal: rust and blades in equal measure. I stride back from the pick-up.

'Don't put her on that! It doesn't look safe.' It's out before I can think.

He repeats it back at me like an eleven-year-old boy, a squeaky version of my voice and a scrunched up irritated face.

'Don't put her on that . . . na naaanaa na na . . .'

Biting my bottom lip. Marching over.

'Look, she could cut herself.'

I lift Frances off and run my hand gently under the bottom of her bare legs for scratches before placing her down on the ground. She looks beseechingly at Mick and the damn plough, wanting to be back there, and he can't resist, playing the kind daddy to my restrictive mum.

'There you go, Frankie, your mother's such a nag.'

I grab his arm as he goes to place Frankie back on it and try to lift her from him. I know it is a mistake to touch him. *She started it.*

'It's not safe,' I try again, 'it might hurt her . . .'

He has Frances under his one arm, clenched against his body, her legs dangling. Her eyes fix on mine, wide and alarmed, but she is silent.

Quietly. As quietly and sweetly as I can.

'Mick, put her down. She looks a bit – worried.'

'Mick, put her down.' Mimicking me again. Heat from the sun is cracking down on the back of my head and I'm dizzy with the strain of keeping calm, of not dropping my eyes from his. Walking beside a scary Alsatian, Dan would whisper to me: never let him know you're scared, that's the trick. They can smell fear at a hundred paces.

'Please. I'm just – worried about Frances getting rust in a cut, she hasn't had a tetanus jab.'

'You are – such – a – fucking – slut.'

'What's this about?' Pretending I don't know. Pretending I didn't know, a week ago, talking to Ryan, enjoying that blissful warm, swimming afternoon that I wouldn't pay for it, sooner or later.

Mick's face close up to mine. Snarling. The top lip raised above the teeth like a wolf.

'Say it. What are you? Slag. I bet you fucked him. You always fuck them.'

'I didn't. I don't know what you're on about . . .' Still trying for a this-is-a-perfectly-normal-situation tone of voice. Still acting like this is an ordinary argument, the kind other couples have, instead of what I know it really is. And underneath, just one tiny thought, not even a thought but a flick-second image: of myself running down the mountain, Frances in my arms, running, screaming *help me* but he'd catch me, he'd catch me, he's faster than me, he'd catch us both.

'Look, give Frances to me. There's no need to scare her, I can see you're in a bad mood, let's talk later about it.'

The sun all around him. He's shining, glowing like hot metal. Keep calm, think about Frances.

I hold out my arms for her.

She has started to whimper. She's only a few inches from me, facing outwards, but around her waist is Mick's arm, clamped. *She's my daughter, you bastard.* Staring into her face is like looking into a mirror. Frances knows what's coming. I might convince myself sometimes that Mick's moods are completely unpredictable, but looking at Frances's wobbly bottom lip and the big, terrified eyes it's clear that one of us knows what is coming next.

'Reeetaa,' she says. She holds out her arms.

'Oh have her, you bloody bitch,' Mick erupts, suddenly thrusting her at me. With the violence of the movement she starts howling and in the next instance he's slapped her, hard across the face.

Everything is tired and broken and dangerous.

'You bastard. Bastard bastard bastard . . .'

I say it quietly and viciously and I am shaking with a shaking which is rattling the ground beneath us, rattling my teeth, rattling Frances's bones. I must take Frances back, take Frances somewhere safe, take Frances to the truck, where can I take Frances? I turn around, suppress the urge to break into a run, start walking, but the back of my neck burns. I know he is behind me.

The second I get to the truck, open the door, start strapping her into the baby-seat, he's at my elbow.

'God I hate you,' he says, into my face, and I know he does, he does, he always has. Say nothing Rita, say nothing, say nothing. Smeary hot tears are dripping onto my arm and Frances is sobbing noisily as I reach for her bottle, my hand shaking as I try to smooth her hair away from her forehead, reach for her mouth with the teat, make soothing sounds, but I can't do it, I can't. *She started it*.

'And I hate *you*, you – violent – no-hope – bastard—'

The first punch is in my back, a fist in the kidneys from behind, which stops me breathing, doubles me up over the bonnet of the truck. Hot metal on my belly. Frances starts screaming.

He pulls me up by the arm to face him and hits me again, this time a punch in the face, dark trees spin in

front of me and my cheekbone crunches like a maca-
roon.

Mummy Mummy Mummy

I'm trying to claw at him – my nails are out – you fight like
a girl Rita, you're useless – I don't know how to inflict pain
on him or stop him as another punch comes flying. His fist
catches me above the eye, rolls my head with a thud against
the side of the truck. My head swings back like a tulip on
a stalk and my bottom lip is hanging open, blood dripping
onto my filthy T-shirt, I can still hear Frances screaming, I
stagger away from the truck, one knee gives way as I try to
run, then he has caught me by the arm, the skin burning
and twisting under his tight grip as he drags me onto the
ground. Stones dig into my back and he puts his face so
close to mine that it isn't a face at all, it is one big, looming,
dark blot: 'You're a whore Rita Barnes – say it! Say it!' His
fist crashes under my ribcage again, I'm folding like a paper
bag, all the air gone from me . . .

I'm a whore

Miles from anywhere, an abandoned museum and a baby
screaming and punches raining on me, on my face, my neck,
my breasts, my stomach.

Not in front of Frances, please, not in front of Frances –

help me

# 20

The night my Dad left. I am six years old, it is a Friday evening in winter. They must have been planning this for months, because all his stuff is mysteriously boxed, appearing from rooms, labelled in blue felt pen. 'TOOLS', 'CAR MANUALS', 'CLEAN SHIRTS' . . . who has done this? Written the labels? He and Mum are silently passing boxes to each other, he puts them in the lift while she keeps her finger on the lift button to hold the door open. There is a van waiting at the bottom of the lifts. A friend of his. A lady friend.

He gives Dan his football magazines, he gives Tony a tiny thumb-planer, the one Tony always used to pinch from his workshop. For Billy he has a signed picture of Jimmy Greaves, but Billy has locked himself in the bathroom. And me? What am I doing? I can't remember. I'm concentrating on the others, and on not being here. I can picture each brother clearly, Tony clinging to Dad's legs; Dan already smoking openly in front of the pair of them, and Billy with his arms tightly wound around his knees, sitting on the bathroom floor. Dad saying over Tony's head to Mum: 'I'll see the boys Saturday after next. Saturday morning,' and neither she nor he notice that he says 'the boys'. The boys.

Later Mum makes us our tea – a thin pizza, from a packet, dry as a red pancake and Billy says: 'I hate your cooking, no wonder my Dad left – I hate you, I hate you!' and scrapes his chair back and runs from the table. He says my Dad, as if he is. Only his. *My Dad.*

I help Mum to clear the table, taking the sauce bottle with the smeary brown top that I always hate to touch and all the plates, including Billy's untouched pizza plate, the pink-handled knives and forks and the pale, bobbly table cloth. I do all this without waiting to be asked, and then I go and watch Mum standing in the kitchen looking out over the flats. Her long brown hair resting on her pinny. Her thin legs in her old slippers, the heels dry as rocks, the toenails painted pink.

A pigeon is messing on the balcony, messing on her washing, but she does nothing. She never moves. She stands really still, looking out over the flats as if my Dad was there somewhere. In one of the windows. In every window there are families. Curtains, lights going off, TVs blinking, people making each other cups of tea, watching the news. It is only in our flat that there is nothing. A blank window with a woman standing stock still in it and a little girl behind her that nobody can see.

Don't cry, Mum. You've still got me, you've still got Rita.

But I know I'm not enough for her. Never will be enough for anyone.

He didn't go for good, my Dad, and only I know this. One night I see his ghost in the living-room and I know he's back. I'm creeping towards the kitchen in my nightie wanting a cup of milk and not daring to ask for one, when I hear voices. My Dad's lovely brown soft voice, my Mum's Angel Whip voice, vanilla. 'Tina,' he says. He is panting. The door of the hatch through the kitchen is slightly open and I can see his big sheepskin coat hanging over the chair, with the dirty fur at the collar like a big sleeping animal. My Mum is making little crying sounds and he says, 'I do love you Tina, I love you girl . . .' I can smell my Dad everywhere; smoke and car fumes and that smell Mum calls 'Bloody

Dagenham' which is something to do with his work, and his lovely clean-soap shaving smell and I know that smell anywhere, I know it's him.

It's late, so late, that's how I know he's a ghost. Even Dan is asleep. There is no electric light, but Mum has taken the nets down to wash them and so I can see the moon through the kitchen window like a saucer of milk; it makes everywhere blue and milky. I daren't go in the living-room and say hello to my Dad, because it will make him disappear, dissolve in a puff of smoke like Rumpelstiltskin when the princess guesses his name. Ghosts don't like you to see them. You have to pretend you didn't. He is sighing. A sea-rushing kind of noise. My Dad is lapping and fading like waves at Southend and when I hear him loudly I want to say Dad, Dad, stay! and then he falls away again and I hear Mum's voice, rising and falling, too. Little sounds. Her quiet voice. One I haven't heard in a long time. Oh Peter. Oh God. I miss you.

I creep back to bed, with his warm voice in my ear. *I love you girl*. I know my Dad loves my Mum, no matter what my Auntie Jackie says. I hear her tell my Mum Pete's a bastard to leave her with four kids to raise and what use was he to her when he was around, anyway? she's better off without him, but I know it isn't true. Of course he loves her. Why else would he sneak back to see her, when we're all asleep? It's us he doesn't love. He's young, with a big wide smile and a gold ring on his little finger made out of a sovereign and a motorbike in the garage that he never has time to do up, and everybody loves him. It's no wonder he left us because money doesn't grow on trees and we never tidy our rooms and we always make a racket when he's trying to watch football on the telly, and I'm the worst because I keep jumping on him when he comes in from work, wanting to wrestle, and don't I know he's had a long hard day and he's knackered and God almighty, Rita, don't you ever leave a poor sod alone for five minutes?

\*    \*    \*

White. Of course it is white when I open my eyes, and pale blue. When I try to turn my head slightly, to focus, I discover my head won't move. There is a blunt pain in my skull, just above my neck. I'm in bed. A sheet is folded down over a blue blanket and my arms are lying flatly on it, crisp as paper arms. I try lifting them – both feel stiff, and the right arm has a bracelet of small purple bruises around the top. Moving my arms makes my breath come in a painful stab.

There are noises, and bright, hot lights, and beds and people. Squeaky trolley wheels and cheerful voices and metal clattering sounds like knives and forks. There is a window opposite me showing one solitary Ponderosa pine tree and searing sunlight. Gingerly, I feel under the sheet. It is my ribs which I now realise are hurting the most, and I discover tight yellow bandages across my breasts and that I am wearing a weird white cotton nightie with only a button at the neck and sleeves and nothing to do it up at the back. Like being at the hairdresser's.

'Hi there. You're awake,' says someone. A young voice, female, and American.

'Can I get you a drink? You need something? To go to the bathroom?'

She is smiling, but she is waiting, not very patiently, and I must say something.

'My – glasses. Could you pass me my glasses?' They are on the table next to the bed but it is not easy for me to stretch for them. I see that she has a nurse's uniform, I know precisely where I am, but I want to prolong the realisation for a moment longer, make a pretence of not-knowing. She hands me the glasses. The room comes more clearly into view. Beds with wheels. A man with a drip in his arm. It is too hot in here, and smells of canteen food and popcorn.

'Reeda. That's right, yes? How you feeling?' Her face swims in front of me. Big eyes. Plump cheeks, a mole just beneath her nose.

She talks too slowly, and I mistrust her voice. False kindness, false concern. 'There's someone waiting to see you. He's anxious. Shall I show him in?'

I try to nod and when that doesn't work, mutter a 'yes'.

Mick appears through the swing doors, his arms full of flowers. The young nurse tactfully slips away, down the ward.

I long to close my eyes. Weight presses on my eyelids.

Mick steps hesitantly towards me to kiss me, and his eyes remind me of Frances; wide and blue and terrified. I accept his kiss on my paper cheek, accept the scratch of his stubble without flinching, and remain still, feeling again the pressure on my eyelids. Then a flicker of alarm.

'Where's Frances?' My voice is croaky. A child's voice, worried.

'Don't worry. I left her with Nancy. She's fine. I didn't want her to see you – like this—'

He covers his eyes with one hand, rubbing at the wrinkles in his forehead with two fingers, and magically, there are tears running over his hands, he leans close to the bed, shaking. Those tears are like a sudden hot spring from the ground; they come from nowhere, but they're copious; look – his hand is already soaking, and they're dripping onto his T-shirt.

My own eyes ache. I watch Mick, fascinated, but remain dry, dry and floating. Perhaps I'm on some kind of medication. Yes, I realise sluggishly, I must be. That explains it.

'There are some tissues on the other side of the bed,' I tell Mick, in a voice which for some reason reminds me of the young nurse. I take my glasses off, place them limply on top of the covers. I can't bear to watch him cry for a moment longer. 'I need a glass of water. I'm parched.'

He reaches for a tissue and now he is sobbing, quiet,

restricted sobbing, trying to catch his breath and talk at the same time.

'I don't know what to do, Rita, tell me what to do.'

'There. On the table. Yes, a big glass. Thank you.'

'Please. Rita, don't be like this. I'm sorry, I'm sorry, I don't know what happens to me . . .'

I'm limp and dry and his emotion washes over me, a deluge.

'Mick. Can you – pass me the water.'

He manages to wipe his eyes and recover himself a little and hands me the glass of water. While I hold the glass he is staring at my lip and fresh tears spring up. I realise when I try to sip that I have no mouth, only a place in my face which is fat and uncontrollable and which dribbles the water back out again. Like being at the dentist. Or in labour. Gas and air, my head is full of it.

'So I look terrible, do I?' I put a hand up to my mouth.

'No, no you look fine,' he says quickly, as if we were going out to dinner and I'd just asked him if he liked my outfit. He cradles the beaker at my bottom lip and tries to tip the water into my mouth. Some reaches the back of my throat and I feel a cold trickle and with an effort, I swallow.

He sits down on the bed, carefully avoiding sitting on my feet. Coughs.

'Rita, what did you say to the doctors?'

His question floats at me. I allow it to hang for a second between us. Again I have an urge to close my eyes, turn my head away. 'I haven't spoken to anyone. I just woke up. I don't even know how I got here.'

'I brought you here.' He's reaching for his cigarettes, then he sees the No Smoking notice and sticks the yellow Top packet back in the pocket of his shorts.

He lowers his voice and leans forward.

'I told them you were attacked. That me and you and

Frances were separated, you went to Old Holson on your own, me and Frankie were in the truck and we went looking at the Wishing Stone.'

'The Wishing Stone. We never got to it.' A limp remark. Pointless. It's hard to hear what he is saying. The sentences float out of his mouth and drift away.

'No, but I told them *I* did. And when I arrived in the truck there you were, badly beaten. Someone had attacked you. I'm sorry – I had to say something.' His blue eyes hold mine and the effort of focusing is exhausting, my eyes are so weary . . .

'So why did you say they attacked me? Was I raped?'

'No you weren't raped. That wasn't the reason.'

'Was I mugged? Was my money gone?'

'No, you weren't mugged. You had no money either.'

'So why then? Why was I attacked?'

My voice is dry, I take another sip of water.

'It was a totally unprovoked attack. Completely motive-less.'

It comes out in a smoky whisper. His face is close to mine. Now he is Mick again, my Mick, the one I know so well and I know that this is a crucial moment; he is asking me for something, asking me quite desperately. His face is close enough to see the hole in the side of his nose where the silver pin used to be. That's how tiny this moment, this possibility, seems to be. A pin-prick hole, already closing up.

I close my eyes and the relief is enormous. My hand rests on the glasses lying on the bed.

'Unprovoked,' I say quietly.

'Yes.'

'Motiveless.'

'Yes.'

When I open my eyes he's staring at me. 'OK,' I murmur. The window with the one Ponderosa tree retreats, shrinks, spins away from me. That's all. The moment is over.

I pull myself up to a sitting position. 'Can you bring Frances to see me? How long do I have to stay in?'

'They haven't said. But it's expensive.'

'What do you mean?'

'Well, paying of course. It isn't like England – I had to fill out all sorts of forms when I brought you in . . .'

I notice for the first time that the T-shirt he is wearing is splatterd with what I had thought were HP sauce stains. Of course they're blood. My blood. This only happened yesterday.

'What's wrong with me?'

'You were concussed. You fell against a rock. They did some X-rays, and they have to wait for the results. But the Doctor said he didn't think there would be any complications.'

He looks down at the flowers; spray carnations in a weak yellow colour, lying in a cellophane wrap, across my body under the blue blanket. Neither of us has suggested putting them in water.

'And two broken ribs. And a hairline crack in your jaw.' His voice softer and softer.

'And my mouth? My mouth hurts. My back hurts. My head hurts.'

'You're on pain-killers. So you can't feel most of it at the moment.'

His eyes light on my arm, on the little ring of bruises. He covers his face in his hands.

'Oh God, Rita. I'm such a shit.'

I feel as flat and papery as the flowers. Nothing matters to me at all. Not that tree out there, not those other people, not Mick crying, not Mick's remorse, not Mick's anger. I care about Frances, but even this is a weak feeling, tucked far away. I only want to sleep.

'I've never done anything like this in my life, you know,

you've got to believe me,' Mick is saying. 'I'll never ever touch you again like this, I swear it, I swear it Rita.'

'How will we pay?'

'What?'

'The hospital bills, how will we pay them? We're not insured, are we?'

He sits up a little. He goes again for his back pocket, remembers, lets his hand fall on the bed. It falls on the flowers.

'I've phoned Jon and Carole. They're on their way here. They'll stay in Sinkalip and help look after Frankie and they'll pay for everything. Don't worry . . .'

Frances. In the heat of the ward I'm almost delirious. I wish he had brought Frances. What can I do about Frances? I don't want her life to be like mine, to have a father who is like the sea, lapping towards her, just wetting the tips of her toes, and then fading away again. To long for him to stay. To make the mistakes I have, searching for him. Frances adores Mick. She'd never forgive me for leaving Mick. I close my eyes again in total exhaustion and never in my life have I wanted it more; to be lost, simply to be lost, to just be lost and to let someone else find me.

'She's still in shock, you know . . .'

That nursy voice again. False, a stage whisper. As if I can't hear her.

'I'll put these flowers in some water for you. Perhaps you'd better leave her now. She could do with some more sleep, I guess.'

The mousy-haired nurse is taking the flowers out of the cellophane and at the same time politely trying to usher Mick out. When he starts sobbing again she puts an arm awkwardly around him and starts walking him towards the door. I watch the glass doors swing behind them.

Shock. Yes. If only I could summon up the energy to even think straight; to shake off this fog. I hear the click of heels as two young nurses come into the room, giggling and whispering.

*Women like that. You just can't help them if they won't help themselves . . .*

## 21

Mick wants to carry me from the truck to the cabin. I'm perfectly capable of walking, it's only the ribs which are still a little tender, but I allow myself to be picked up, link my hands behind his neck. I'm light as a doll, as a tiny girl. Frances runs at our feet, thwacking Mick's legs with a Ponderosa twig.

'Eyes closed,' orders Mick, 'it's a surprise!'

'Supwise, supwise,' chants Frances. She's picking up on a mood; bristling, nervous. I want to lean down and scoop her up into my arms, but I do as Mick says, close my eyes, let my legs swing, feeling his arm tight under my thighs, slippery with sweat. Even in the two weeks I've been away, Frances has changed, those amazing infinitesimal changes that babies make; a hardening of the edges around the chin, the nose has grown a fraction of a centimetre, the eyebrows are the merest shade darker, but you can tell. When you know your child's face this well, you can almost see the cells shifting and regrouping.

Mick pants as he strides determinedly up the steps to the deck. A pause while he messes around with the lock, pulling the door towards us. I screw my eyes tight and breathe in the smell of sweat and the smoky-wood smell of the cabin. Once inside, with a bit of staggering he manages to put me down on the sofa.

'Keep them eyes closed, doll, it isn't quite ready.'

I know this mood. Contrite. But not necessarily safe. I am aware of a hissing water sound and the fact that it is hot in here, hotter than outside. From the crackling and the smell it's obvious the stove is on. Orange light flickers on my closed eyelids.

He is lighting a match. The sound of striking and Frances saying 'Lighter! Lighter!' The smell of candle wax.

'One more minute,' Mick says, 'then you can open your eyes . . .'

He's taking my shoes off. I sit up and allow him to undo the trainers and Frances says 'pooh stinky' and then Mick says, 'Stand up,' and he begins to pull my T-shirt over my head, but I clutch at it and before I can stop myself blurt, 'What? What are you doing?'

'Trust in me . . .' he drawls playfully, in his voice like the snake from *Jungle Book*. I let him take my T-shirt off and help to pull down my shorts.

'Mummy's knickers!' squeals Frances in delight.

I'm standing up now and I lean on Mick as I pull them down and I'm struggling with this desire, the dizzy tingling in the roof of my mouth. I mustn't feel these feelings in the daytime with Frances here, and I mustn't feel them now, especially.

'Sit down again,' Mick says.

My bare skin on the rough sofa. The sound of Mick going over to the stove and some slopping water sounds and him saying sharply to Frances 'Stay near Mum, that's dangerous'.

Mick's footsteps come back, he's standing in front of me and my nipples pop out like eyes on stalks but he doesn't touch them, instead he bends down and picks me up again.

'Open!' he says, and I do.

We have a bathroom. In one corner of the cabin he has

made a partition out of plyboard. Instead of a door there is an old green velvet curtain on a piece of wire. The logs have been properly stripped and filled in between with this chalky white stuff and chicken wire. He has rigged up a shelf with Gee Your Hair Smells Terrific and Barbasol Beardbuster and Lava soap and a flannel. And in the centre is the old tin bath with the rusty edges that we strapped to the truck and brought all the way from Mount Vernon.

It's the sight of that bath. Tears spring into my eyes.

A murmur of pain in my ribs. Mick is watching my face, he needs something from me, and if I could just give it, just this once, everything would be over, be finally all right.

'It's lovely, Mick.' My skin is goose-pimpled. I summon up a smile and he beams back.

On each corner of the bath is a candle on a saucer. The bath is plugged with something which looks like two teats from Frances's bottle stuck inside each other. Steam rises in clouds and a towel is folded neatly on the floor beside the bath.

'How does it drain out?' I step onto the folded towel.

'I've made a hole in the corner and run stove piping under the cabin and away down the incline. I'll show you after.'

'Won't it be really cold in winter? With a big hole under the bath?'

'Oh, worry about that later, Miss Worry-Wart.' The goose-pimples are drawing together, I'm starting to shiver. I make a move to get in.

'Let me put you in.'

Mick puts his arms under me. I smile swiftly, my eyes on Frances.

She is watching intensely as Mick crouches to pick me up again, dangles my toes into the water to check it isn't too hot, then lowers me in.

'Fwankie bath!' she says, tearing at her own clothes. The

shoes are off and the T-shirt before I've even got my shoulders wet.

'OK, honey-pie,' says Mick, gently helping her to unpeel the tabs on her nappy. Her matted hair sticks to her head and her body is covered in grey smears, mosquito bites and scratches from the trees. She is brown everywhere except where the nappy was and little white socks from keeping her trainers on.

'Hot!' she squawks, unable to sit down in it.

'How did you heat the water?' I ask.

'On the stove of course . . .' Mick smiles, showing me the tin baby bath he put on top of the stove. 'We can't have it very deep, though. This has used up tons.'

He goes behind the partition and reappears with a plastic tumbler.

'Champagne. Welcome home, doll.' He hands it to me. Up close he whispers.

'I'm sorry. You know I love you.'

Champagne dribbles onto my chest. The bruises everywhere are a brown-banana yellow with a tinge of blue. I'm still on pain-killers but the Doctor says the ribs will heal in a couple of weeks, there's no need to stay in hospital now they know my head is fine. My body looks thin and foreign to me; browner than it's ever been and, despite the out-of-proportion tits, more boyish. Only the big dark nipples to say that this is a woman's body, a body that's fed a baby. But not my body.

Frances is splashing. Her cheeks are red and her curls damply plastered around her neck. One candle sizzles out as she splashes water onto it. A tiny spider runs along the log nearest the bath edge and Frances splashes that too.

'She's missed you,' Mick is standing in the doorway, smoking, turning his head to blow the smoke outwards towards the cabin rather than in the bathroom with us. It's dark now without one of the candles. It is only afternoon but there's no window in here.

Frances chuckles manically. Now she is splashing me, gently at first. Then more determinedly. Water flies up into my face. Frances shrieks in pleasure. Smack smack, her little hands in the water.

'Careful Frankie,' I warn, as she splashes harder. *Smack* on the surface of the water.

'Mind Mummy's – ribs—'

I say, as a flat little palm comes flying right at me so hard that I scream, leap up, grab her by the upper arms, swing her out of the bath, swilling water everywhere, and smack her right back, slap her hard across the bottom, a stinging thwack which makes her scream, and then another whack across the legs and then another . . .

You – fucking – little – bitch—

'Rita, for God's sake!' Mick's tone is so shocked that I know I've done something wrong, something out of proportion but I can't think straight, I can't see anything, rage is steaming up from my ankles to my face, he struggles to free Frances from the snapped-tight grip of my hand around her arm, he's saying 'She didn't mean it, it was an accident,' and she is screaming right into my face and my ribs are cracking with pain, aching, aching.

'She hates me,' I'm sobbing. 'I'm sick to death of her. Everything I do – she doesn't respond to me – she's always – picking – on – me – I try and try – to love her – but . . .' The words won't come out, between the sobs, my mouth is full of the rage and it's like foam, it's like a hive of bees, it won't let me speak, it makes me giddy.

Mick is prising at my fingers around her arm, shaking me loose.

'Go upstairs and lie down. Fuck's sake. Have a sleep or something – go on, upstairs!'

His tone is harsh enough to get through to me; I stagger upstairs, dripping wet footprints everywhere as I slump up to our bedroom, goose-pimples breaking out all over my skin, and shivering despite the warmth in the cabin. I hear Frances's crying dying down, reducing to an occasional gulp and an occasional whine and Mick is softly comforting her, 'There there, Frances, naughty Mummy isn't well, Daddy will tell her off later, there there darling . . .'

I bury my face in the pillow and now the rage is pouring out of me like blood. It seeps away out into the cool dirty sheet and the logs and into the darkening afternoon sky outside. I'm limp and hollow and I hate myself.

In the night, the dream again. Mick, glorious, tanned, strong, his beautiful, muscular, furred chest, the defined undulating curves of his arms and calf-muscles, the prominent pointed ankle bones. He is standing on top of the small boulder. The one he wants to blast for gold. Hands in the pockets of his shorts. The sun behind him, shining through his hair. A raven flies over. And I'm creeping behind him, behind the rock, I'm on all fours so that he won't see me. Knock knock knock. I have the hammer, but it is a giant hammer, as big as me. I carry it in my teeth. It drags on the ground, knock knock knock. But he doesn't hear it. He doesn't see me stand up. He doesn't feel me climb up. Until I am right beside him, I'm taller than him, I've grown towering, taken right off, my feet are off the ground, off the rock completely, I'm suspended with the giant hammer right above his head, metal and wood, heavy, heavier than me. I raise it in both arms. I bring it down. KNOCK KNOCK KNOCK. Mick falls sideways, and his bones crunch against the rock as he falls, slides off the rock, leaving a red clotted smear, like berries and juice.

I wake with Mick sprawled beside me, on his stomach, the sheets tangled round his legs. I'm cold. It's late but there is bright moonlight; the trees through our window are frosted in blue. I've woken flooded with guilt.

Crying woke me. I thought it was Frances but now I lie on my back, listen harder and realise that it is outside. I sit up.

I find a T-shirt beside the bed and leggings and Mick's socks and I put them on.

I pad carefully down the ladder, slippy in my socked feet. I don't need the candle, the blue light is strong enough to see by.

Frances is sleeping downstairs in her travel cot. Mick has put her to bed in just her nappy and her skin feels cool to the touch; also he forgot the mosquito net, which is in a heap on the floor beside the cot. I unfold it and lay it carefully on top of the high-framed cot, pegging the edges to keep it there. The crying outside continues, and Frances turns over in her sleep.

Coyote, I tell myself. The howls rise like smoke, long, undulating. Nothing to worry about. Wild dogs, that's all. A breeze creeps along my arm; every hair pricks up.

If only I could see one, just this once. That would be better. In this light it would be possible. When I've seen one, I'll know. I take a long deep breath. I carefully push open the cabin door.

The howls are all around the cabin, but I can't see anything move. My breath is coming in short pants, like a dog. I'm listening with every nerve in my body. Now a sound is behind me to the left; now down there by the gravel road, now far down the mountain, now near Nancy and Jim's place. The howls toss back and forth, from one creature to another. This is how they communicate, didn't I read that, surrounding prey, cutting off escape routes.

Something dark swoops and dives above the treetops; I catch my breath. A bat. Each tree is picked out in a milky blue, and utterly still. A hunter's moon. Perfect light to hunt by.

I can't understand how Mick and Frances are sleeping. How they can't hear this. My mouth is dry, my neck and head are aching and I'm straining to see something, staring at every tree for a dark shape, every rock for a sign of movement. Splashes of yarrow on the grass near the truck. A plastic carrier bag of old nappies, a rip saw hanging from a tree by a nail, way out of Frances's reach. Blue all of them. Not a flicker.

The mountain is alive with howling and it seems like I'm the only one in the world who can hear it.

From inside the cabin Frances makes a whimper, only a faint sound, but I jump out of my skin. I must have been frozen in this position for a full five minutes; was my heart even beating? The fear which was in my skin, in my tongue, has retreated to my chest, I feel it lodge there as I go back into the cabin, refusing to be soothed, even when the howls ebb down the mountain.

I try padding upstairs and curling up against Mick's hot back. But that doesn't work, the pounding in my chest continues. So I go back downstairs and stare at Frances through the pegged mosquito net. For a moment I remember the first time I saw her, really looked at her properly. Waking, groggy, in the overheated maternity ward in the middle of the night to find her there beside me in a plastic box beside the bed, scrunched up and foreign, like a new pet, a hamster. Staring in disbelief at that hamster, with its ugly, red, screwed-up face. So here you are. So here's what it all came to, what it amounts to. This.

But then the weird little hamster opens one crusty eye. One eye, blue and shaped like a fish swims around in the tiny face and suddenly the face looks like Frances. Like a person. Like me. And the rush of love, the moment I think of as my waters breaking. Not a physical thing. A rush. A flood. A sensation so powerful it could hardly be called a sensation at all, or an emotion. It cracked at the walls of my ribcage, ripped through me. This feeling didn't come from outside of me, it was in me all this time, how could I not know I had it until now?

I do love you Frances, I do, I do. I don't know what comes over me, I'm such a terrible, horrible mother, I'm sorry, I'm sorry. Frances. My darling blonde girl, my baby girl, my only girl. I love you so much. I'll never smack you again Frances. I promise.

# 22

In the morning Mick ties balloons to the trees; Carole and Jon are coming up to the cabin to say goodbye to us before they drive back to Mount Vernon. They have been staying in the Red Apple Motel in Sinkalip for a while. They came to the hospital every day; brief, awkward visits, with Carole studiously avoiding any reference to the 'attack' and intercepting Frances's curiosity and questions about my bandaged ribs with a hasty 'sssh now – don't upset Mom'.

I feed Frances soggy Cheerios from a bowl washed in last night's bath-water. We are outdoors on the deck, she is strapped into her buggy; in the absence of a high chair this is the easiest way to feed her. The buggy is covered in caked-on porridge and other stuff so maybe I'll give up this method soon. Perhaps it's easiest to let her wander around and come back for a spoonful every half hour. Children never starve themselves, that's what my Mum would say. As I aim another spoonful at her mouth she squirms and turns her head away, so I give up and unstrap her.

'OK Frances, do it your way.' My voice is tired and defeated. A squirrel runs along the roof, squawking noisily. A huge, ugly squirrel, long-bodied like a ferret and a nasty orangey-grey colour; must be a Douglas, the same one that woke me this morning. Frances and I watch it run down the logs of the cabin, speed along the nearest Lodge pole and disappear.

'It's going to its nest,' I tell her, trying for a different voice, a cheerful voice. She stands staring at me, carefully licking the milk from around her mouth with a slow pink tongue.

'Squirrel,' I say.

She says nothing.

There is the sound of a car engine. Mick ties the last red balloon around the branches of a Tamerack and then reaches in his shorts pocket for his tobacco. I watch Frances run down the drive towards him, in her bright yellow T-shirt and green stripy shorts. Although I'm staring at the back of her head I somehow know she is grinning.

Carole and Jon pull up. I notice that they brought the Toyota – must have been thinking of all this rough terrain. Didn't want to ruin the Saab.

The lanky figure of Carole unfolds awkardly from the car, the strap of her handbag across her chest as she gets out on the same side as Mick, waving up to me and giving him a peck on the cheek. She has long tanned legs and expensive trainers, but no natural elegance. Carole's four years older than me but she reminds me of one of those girls in the year below at school. Good at netball. Knows nothing about boys. Still doesn't know how to use eye-liner and that you should never wear a black bra under a white T-shirt.

I have on the daisy dress but no make-up and I haven't looked in a mirror since I left hospital, so I suppose I'm a fine one to talk right now. I can tell from touching that my swollen lip has reduced down quite a bit but I've no idea what it looks like. What my face looks like. I know from the way Frances reacted to me when she woke up this morning, before she had remembered, that I must look pretty strange. I push my glasses up to my nose and think what bliss it is not to know. I suppose I could look in the wing-mirror of the truck; but why bother?

'Hi there, Rita,' says Jon, sticking his head out of the car window. He's trying to turn the car around so he can back up and park behind our truck. Mick is directing him, standing near the problem rock that we always have to avoid, the one that Mick has tried to dig out and failed. You can tell Jon is nervous. That Toyota doesn't have a scratch on it.

Carole puts her arm around me.

'You're looking much better. How you feeling, honey?'

I say I'm feeling fine.

Their boy, Martin, is pulling faces at Frances from the car window. Jon finally manages to park and climbs out, first opening the door for Martin to get out, then carefully locking both car doors behind him.

Mick cracks up laughing.

'Who do you think's going to nick your car out here, eh?'

Jon smiles sheepishly.

'Force of habit, I guess. Even out here in the boonies . . .'

Jon's accent is much more American than Mick's, but their voices are the same, same pitch, same roughness around the edges. Jon smokes too, which might have something to do with it.

'That's quite a climb – how many miles up are we?' Jon asks and Mick tells him four and a half thousand feet and they both make this whistling sound with their teeth, then laugh. Yes they are alike, but those chiselled features, those bright blue eyes look better on Mick; he's got the big nose and the thick eyebrows and the hard jaw-line that stops it all turning to girly pap. Jon is younger, and a fraction shorter and blonder. I've heard Mick say that he looks more like their mother.

The day is gorgeous. A blooming, twittering day with sun-light so dazzling that Frances running around in it is like one big dandelion clock on a yellow and green stalk. We take Carole and Jon on a short tour of our seven acres;

the rocky bit where Mick is certain he could blast some gold, the incline down to the 'valley' where Mick wants to drill another well; the place behind the trees where Mick wants to build another house eventually; and a tiny clump of tigerlilies I found, only yesterday, growing behind the out-house; a patch of vivid orange heads scattered like spilled paprika.

'You sure have your work cut out for you,' Carole says, picking her way through the deer-brush.

Frances is attempting to carry a stick that she's found, she's mimicking Mick, who also carries a long branch of Ponderosa, and pokes at mushrooms and interesting holes with it. In her efforts to be like Mick she is falling behind us and having thwacked Martin once, accidentally, I offer to carry it for her. She screws up her face.

'No – Fwankie do it!' she says.

'Her speech is coming on great,' comments Carole, 'how old is she now?'

It takes me a moment to work it out.

'Twenty-one months. Nearly two.'

'Wow. Martin couldn't say much at that age.' Martin is in front of us, hands in pockets, walking behind the two men. Six or seven, to me he is a typical American boy; cropped brown hair framing a round face, he looks like he's been raised on high quality beef and ridiculously large vegetables. I can never look at Martin without remembering a conversation I had with Carole when we first got to Mount Vernon – when I first met her – when she asked me if Mick was circumcised. 'I can never forget my *horror*' (she says 'horror' like Dolly Parton would; like a blonde sexpot who is Southern innocence personified) 'when I found out that Jon hadn't had that snip. I guess you English don't worry about it, do you, but I made sure Martin had the operation. It's so much more *hygienic* . . .'

And when I'd recovered myself enough to say that Mick

wasn't circumcised either – that apparently it was their father, Michael Senior, who refused to let the Doctors do it – she gave me such a look of kindred suffering that it was all I could do to keep from laughing. I told Mick about it later and he held my hand over his cock and asked me 'now wouldn't you miss that sweet little wrinkly bit at the end, and doing *that*,' (moving my hand) and then he said more seriously, 'Americans are barbaric, it's like taking an eyelid off,' and of course he grew big in my hand and I had to agree I did like it because it was like unpeeling an ice-pop and I couldn't imagine Mick without that protective little skin; couldn't bear to imagine how vulnerable he'd be.

Carole has stopped, sitting on a tree-stump to take her trainer off and tip out a stone. Frances is watching a tiny blue butterfly descend on a small rock. I can see that she is puzzled by the fact that when it holds its wings together the underwing is brown and blends with the rock – it disappears; when it opens the wings it appears again. I'm amazed that Frances has the sense to keep very still, but then it occurs to me it probably isn't sense, she's genuinely mesmerised.

A tap tap on a tree to our right makes all three of us look up.

'Wow. Pileated woodpecker. Look at that,' I shade my eyes to stare up at it and Carole does the same. 'It's the biggest woodpecker in America – there does seem to be a pair round here because I've seen it before . . .' I stop, realising that I sound like Mick. Carole has laced up her trainer. I suddenly notice that she is not staring up at the woodpecker at all, but at me. Mick and Jon have reached the cabin; we can see them on the deck about 200 yards away, because we're higher up than them, we're on the other side of a dip in the land, a kind of small valley.

'Does he hit you?'

Carole's low voice is like a piece of gravel. That's exactly it – she just threw a stone at me.

'What?'

'Mick – does he hit you?'

I look at Frances. I glance at the woodpecker with its weird black eye mask and its long sharp beak, poking and prodding.

'I—'

Carole glances from me to Frances and lowers her voice still further.

'Because, if he does, you know, you don't have to take that shit from any man . . .'

She sounds like something from Oprah Winfrey. 'Wake up and smell the coffee.' I don't know what to say but I feel a surge of anger, a small fury as I manage at last, to look back at Carole, see her sitting there with her smug ironed shorts, her neat white trainers and her perfect American smile that never stretched itself over a cock that wasn't scrubbed and pared like an apple and scented with soap. Everyone thinks they'd know what to do. That there are two types of women; those who put up with shit and those – themselves – who don't.

'What makes you think – that?' I say, at last.

Her tone is matter of fact now, she can't look me in the eye.

'Just concern, honey. You know about Jon's Mom – I mean Jon and Mick's Mom.'

'Yes . . .' I lie, 'but what's that got to do with it?'

'They —' she's uncertain now, I can see it, but she marches on regardless, keeping her voice low so that Frances doesn't hear. Martin is on the other side of the valley, walking up towards the cabin.

'They do say you know, boys raised in an atmosphere of violence – they say they grow up to do the same. Beat their women. You know – a circle of abuse that repeats itself.'

'I did a year's therapy course. I know all that,' I say sharply. My voice is calm but my heart is knocking at my ribcage. Tap tap tap.

'Well, it's just that – I used to wonder if Jon would ever turn out like that – like his father – and it scared me.'

'Jon?'

I push my glasses onto my nose with one finger, glance over to our cabin, see from here that Mick and Jon are sitting on two chairs on the deck, drinking beer.

'But he isn't – Jon isn't, never has been, he doesn't have much of a temper. In fact,' – a wry laugh, here, a joke at her own expense – 'if anything it's me who has the temper, Jon just caves in. Like his mother. Jon's the one who was most like Cherie-Rose.'

Her voice has become almost inaudible. The red crest of the woodpecker flickers as its head pecks on.

Carole runs a hand through her shiny blonde hair, pushing it away from her ears where it falls back instantly. Not a hair out of place. Like hair in TV ads.

'Such a terrible thing to do. How could you leave two lovely boys like that? Could you ever do it?'

Her eyes shine. The bright sunlight must be making them water.

'Leave them?' My voice now as quiet as hers.

'I feel so sad for Jon sometimes, you know that?' She brushes a wet streak from her cheek. 'Even now he's twenty-eight, he's like a boy. He misses her so much. Maybe it's something to do with me being those couple of years older than him. I know I shouldn't mother him, but do you find yourself doing that?' I shake my head and she carries on, not needing a response.

'It's real hard not to, take a – mothering role – when you know their own mother had such a diabolical life, and killed herself when she was – exactly your age.'

'Tap tap tap!' screeches Frances, losing interest in the butterfly and pointing to the woodpecker. Her voice is so sudden and high-pitched that the huge bird sees us at last, and takes flight.

'Poor Cherie-Rose,' Carole says, brushing her shorts with her hands as she stands up. She puts an arm around me and doesn't seem to notice my stiffness, my silence. 'Poor Jon and Mick. What a sad thing for two boys, to lose their mother like that. I hope I didn't offend you, honey? Asking you about Mick? It's just something I used to worry about myself. About Jon, you know. But Jon's real soft. Like a kitten. I'm sure Mick is the same.'

'And if he wasn't,' she adds, as we're walking up the incline, pushing small sprouting Ponderosas out of our way with Frances's stick, 'I know you'd get the hell out of here. I know we don't know each other real well. But I can see that right off. You're not the kind that would stay.'

She pushes her swinging hair away from her face again. I'm beside her, I see for a moment her face in profile; but I can't decide, I just can't decide from looking at her. She might be telling the truth. She might be saying exactly what she thinks, I might have convinced her that Mick would never do anything violent, that I knew all about Cherie-Rose's suicide, that I can look after myself.

There again, in her own clumsy way, who knows? Perhaps Carole likes me. Perhaps she was even trying to help.

# 23 ∫

Mick at ten years old. This is how I imagine Mick at ten years old. He looks like an older version of Frances; blonde, round face, a basin cut, big blue eyes; a sweet, feminine face with only the definition around the chin and jaw to suggest the face he has now. And of course, no big nose, that's something men grow, like stubble.

Sweet-natured too. I'm convinced of it. Mick is two years older than Jon – making Jon eight in this picture. We're in the States of course. Somewhere I don't know. Mick grew up in a funny little town called Waukesha, Wisconsin, and he tells me now how the locals pronounced it with the 'a' dragged out for five seconds and the mouth stretched wide to accommodate the vowel sounds; WAAAAKAAASHAAAA . . . Even at ten, I bet he was a great mimic.

This is now I imagine Waukesha. It probably has a JC Penny's and a Seven-Eleven, and a Woolworth's with a long counter where you can sit on stools with chrome stands and order a Malt or a Chocolate Milk or a steamed milk with honey and almond. Kids eat Twinkies and Snickers bars and go to summer camp (or is that only middle-class America? Not sure if I can quite fit Mick's family into this picture); well if not summer camp they go to festivals in Milwaukee called SummerFest, and the Mums who are called 'Moms' take the kids on picnics; make baskets out of watermelon, packed with neat pink chunks of fruit, and bring cool boxes of 7-Up and make their own sour cream and chive dip. There's a small church and a First Federal Bank of Waukesha, with a sign outside that tells you the temperature on any given day, and there are houses with long sloping lawns outside, and no fences or hedges, and men wearing short-sleeved cream and navy baseball shirts and baggy shorts, mow lawns on them. It's summer, and I got all this from books and from *Happy Days* where the Fonz mentioned Waukesha once and that was the fifties, when teenagers were invented. Mick was born in 1961.

This must be the summer of 1971. Mick is ten. His Dad likes soul and listens to the Isley Brothers, Diana Ross and the Chilites, nothing too 'heavy' or 'deep' – he doesn't like Aretha. Michael Senior is handsome; thicker set than Mick is now, taller, darker, with only the profile, the nose and perhaps something in the grin to connect him to Mick. He is an engineer, he came to the States from Nottingham, adventuring, working first at Mount Vernon on logging machinery. This is where he met Cherie-Rose. He came to the mid-West with his young wife and two kids, to work at a paper plant.

Cherie-Rose. Fine brown hair, she wears 'bangs' and just a hint of coral lip gloss. Slim, possibly too slim, she looks younger than her twenty-six years, with a wide-eyed expression quite wrong for her steely temperament, her tough beginnings.

Pregnant at sixteen, she left school a promising A student to marry Michael, the handsome foreigner, the English boy, ten years older than her. I remember a photograph Mick showed me. There she is, a trim, youthful figure in her Levi flares, a flowered apron tied over the jeans, hugging two boys who are already up to her ribcage.

But something doesn't fit. This beautiful Cherie-Rose Mom, too young and too bright to be saddled with two boys before the age of twenty, is also someone else. Something about her in his stories and anecdotes that Mick still doesn't understand. A particular expression in photographs, or the way she is standing; something which explains memories of Mick's where she would come into his bedroom at night, carefully pack a small bag of his things, hide it under the bed while he pretended to sleep, and then at the sound of a light switch being turned on in the hall, would jump and scuttle out.

There is a hospital stay, once, short, but he isn't allowed to visit her and there are things in the mornings which end up broken; her favourite vase, a wall covered in ketchup, another time, curtains torn down. Late at night Cherie-Rose sometimes tiptoes out to a neighbour's, and Mick watches at the window, burying his face in the drapes, while the shadowy mother slips across the lawn. Sometimes she seems to be laughing; the way she holds her hand up to her mouth, the way her shoulders are shaking.

And other things, but he doesn't want to think about those. Again, at night there are arguments; yelling, bumps and sounds like furniture being turned over, and Mick and Jon are told never, never on any account to come downstairs after bedtime. The strange part is, they never do. No matter what the noise, the cryings, once a long prolonged scream, they never do go downstairs. And Mick doesn't know why.

That is, he can't tell me why. I think he knows why. I think he dreams about it.

'Mick?'

Carole and Jon have long gone. We've picked up the beer cans and bundled them into a black plastic bin liner and dumped the plates in the washing-up bowl, leaving it on the deck for the chipmunks to clean up. We've turned out the lamp and the extinguished flame makes a singing hiss all around the cabin, and we're snuggled upstairs in our heavily blanketed bed and Mick is kissing me.

'What?' Mick says, planting another kiss on my throat, my collar bone, reaching under the covers to lift up my T-shirt but stifled by my gasp, my 'mind my ribs!' he stops in mid-kiss. There is a pause, then I venture: 'Carole told me something about your Mum. About Cherie-Rose.'

His head emerges from under the blankets. I lie there with the nerves in my body pulled tight.

'Don't be angry.' I stroke his head. He holds it very still. The hissing stops and the cabin is silent.

'OK,' Mick says, his voice muffled, his head down under the covers again. 'I lied. What difference does it make?'

'I don't know. Not much. I don't know why you didn't tell me though, when we first met? I mean, *how* she died . . .'

The weight of his head on my breast-bone. Like lead. I feel him clamber up onto me and desire flickers along my body. I shift slightly, support myself on my elbows so that his weight is eased from my chest, but the desire flickers and dies down. I'm as still and pliant as a field of moss.

He makes love like he is searching for a seam, a place to let me out. Or maybe to crack me open. In any case, he doesn't find it, and he comes long before I'm ready, so that when he rolls over he lies like a dead weight beside me, drawing all the oxygen in the room to his side of the bed. I'm left staring at nothing, at darkness, I feel pummelled and worked and heaved and drilled and flung about, like sand, like dust, until not one bit of me is left.

Cherie-Rose. I know Cherie-Rose. Here she is waking; it's seven a.m., she needs no alarm, what wakes her is the knowledge that she must get up, make coffee, get both boys out of bed and fed and ready for school, and all without disturbing Michael.

Michael Senior is working shifts at the paper plant. He needs his sleep, he needs to sleep late, and if he does, that will make the day bearable. Cherie-Rose has a shiny gown of nylon with pink roses on a cream background. She slips this around her slight frame, ties the knot tightly. In the kitchen the shades are up. She doesn't want Michael to accuse her of flaunting herself to the neighbours.

She makes good strong coffee, real coffee, in a pot which is her pride and joy. She loves the shape of it, the lip with its slight curl, the tall slim shape, the pattern of dainty black and white checks. Usually Cherie-Rose likes things with flowers on. Roses mostly. Pinks are good, peaches better and hot-pink best of all. But this morning nothing can please her more than that coffee pot. She pours the strong brown liquid into her cup, mourns briefly the matching cups that Michael smashed one time, each narrowly missing her head, and then squashes the thought. Ten after seven. Time is running on. But she can't seem to shift herself.

The hot coffee runs down her throat. She hears the refuse-truck in the street, a few shouts from the guys working it. She pads down the corridor on bare feet to look in on the boys. She should wake them, she doesn't know why she isn't waking them.

Mick is curled with his bottom lip jutting out, his blond hair sweating slightly at the fringe, tangled where he has pushed it away from his eyes in sleep. Ten years old. He is filling out, looks less like her and more like his father. This thought causes Cherie-Rose pain.

She steps lightly over to Jon, but doesn't touch him. The back of his head is to her, the sheet pulled up to his ear. He has a smell which is sweet, pink, a smell of Bazooka-Joe bubblegum. She insists he brushes his teeth in front of her every night but maybe he sneaks them under his pillow to chew in bed after lights are out. She worries about the gum, maybe he'll fall asleep one time and choke on it. She thinks of mentioning it to Michael; winces, pain twists in her stomach, and then deadness again.

Back to the kitchen. *I must wake the boys.* It is a thought but it comes unbidden, she has no intention of heeding it. There is bliss in the silence of the house. She can hear her nylon robe rustling when she crosses her leg. She examines curiously the knee which peeps out from between the robe; a knee with freckles, a brown, young-looking knee, with light blonde hairs, is that her knee? She drains the coffee and the liquid going down is slow, warm, she feels it trickle inside her chest; it ought to revive her but it doesn't. She thinks calmly and briefly that it is the last thing she will ever taste, and that curiously, this coffee pot and this cup of coffee is the first thing in a long time that has given her pleasure. She considers writing a note for the boys. This thought brings a picture of both much younger; Jon trying to punch his father at the age of four, yelling 'Leave her alone, I hate you, I hate you . . .' and Mick looking on, standing in the doorway, six years old, rigid, tears streaming down his face, standing stock still, not hating his father, but her, for being unable to prevent it.

Dear boys. I love you both very much. Your Mom will always love you. Please don't be too hard on me, and know how much I tried to stay with you both . . .

She decides against the note. She is tired of explanations, of the feeling that she can never explain.

She fingers the roses on her gown, wonders if she should be wearing something else? She had no idea when she woke up that this would be the day, but now she knows, she knows with absolute certainty that the dead weight inside her cannot be cracked open. It is over. She is over.

With the first paracetamol she remembers the bruises, a pattern like violet pansies along her ribcage, travelling down to her thighs. Strange that they have not been hurting this morning, especially since they are so fresh. With the last glass of water she remembers with a feeling far away that is perhaps pain, that now the boys will see them, or even the police, and what explanation will Michael give?

# 24

Today Mick starts work in the apple valley in Goldtown. Jim comes by in the truck to pick him up; he's all dark shades and back-slapping with a big bag of grass in his back pocket, so somehow I don't think they're off for a day of hard graft.

I watch them from the deck of the cabin with Frances on my hip. A quick kiss from Mick and a 'See you later doll,' and then I'm left. Watching the dust fly up from the back wheels as Jim reverses over a tree-stump and bounces down the pine-cone drive.

I could burst into tears and I don't know why.

'Just you and me love, isn't it?' I say. Cheery voice.

Frances squirms in my arms to be put down.

A whole day ahead of us. God knows what time it is, and what time they'll be back. I'm used to time on my hands, all those months on the dole, time isn't a problem to me like it is to some people. It's not that. It's being left.

I go inside and chop Frances and me a piece of soft honeydew melon. I watch her bite it in excitement, squirting juice over her mucky little chin and know that I must look just as sticky and grimy and my hair just as chewed-up.

'I think we need a visit to Top Lake. Give Frankie a wash, eh? Mum can leave all that nasty work until another day, eh Frankie?'

The nasty work is Mick's task for me. Stripping the bark

from the logs. I spent most of yesterday chipping with a chisel and peeling and tugging and my hands are blistered and raw. The cabin now sits on a nest of broken up bark and chippings which I haven't got round to clearing yet. Lazy. I'm lazy and useless Mick says and he doesn't know why I came here if I don't intend to make it work. Once I would have argued with him.

I strap Frances in the buggy, the walk would be too much for her. She clutches a pink teether cup of juice in one hand and chews on the head of her Sindy doll. I sling a bag of sun-cream, bug repellent, apples, bread, water, towel, sun-hat; the usual stuff in a carrier bag and hang it over the handle of the buggy. Frances pulls Sindy out of her mouth for a moment to make a long, noisy sighing noise and I realise with a start that she is mimicking me.

Top Lake looks different today. The yellow flowers on the lily pads have dried into burnt brown bundles, and the lake wears a dark-green skin. Uninviting. The circle of trees in the middle of the water have reduced still further to grey skeleton trees, and the Tameracks dotted between the pines around the lake are bright splashes of yellow – a harsh note among the deep soft green that I remember.

Overhead noisy ravens and one huge bird with red under its wings that I used to think was an eagle. Now I know it's just an oversized chicken-hawk.

I lay my towel on the grass and wheel the buggy up to a flat spot near the water's edge, putting the brake on with my foot. Then I move it back a few feet. Frances is sleeping. Her head lolls over to one side. I rig up a canopy with my T-shirt over the handles of the buggy, to keep the sun off her and then gently rub a little of the mosquito-zap on her exposed skin.

Apart from the birds it is deserted. No beer cans or signs of recent tyre marks, so I strip off.

The bruises across my ribs have changed colour again. This

time they are a dirty brown with lemon around the edges. They look worse now than when they were fresh. But they don't hurt. Soon they'll be gone. I rest my hands on them. I feel my heart beating but even though it's normal, it unnerves me; fast or slow, it's got so that I can't stand it, I feel like I'm holding a frightened bird. I rest my hands on my sweaty hips. I reek of the lavender cream.

I stand at the water's edge for a long time searching for snakes, watching the violet tails stick onto any stalks they can find, pushing up through the water. I think about Cherie-Rose. What does it take to commit suicide when you have two children? Like Sylvia Plath. The bit that always bothered me was that she left the children milk and a sandwich in case they woke in the night and found her gone. Found her gone. What on earth does that mean? How can you find someone if they have already gone?

I go back to where Frances is sleeping and place my glasses on the top of my T-shirt canopy. Without them I can't see Frances's flickering eye-lids, the fact that she is having a dream. I can't wonder what her dream is about. Or remember my own dreams, scary dreams, wonder why I haven't had them lately. They have been replaced by dreams about Cherie-Rose.

What options are there? I place one foot tentatively into the water. Icy cold, even in this heat. My toes touch stones and melting earth.

Cherie-Rose, couldn't you just have left him?

Where could I go? He would find me. He threatened to find me, wherever I went. He said he'd kill me. He'd never let me take the boys.

Didn't you have family? Didn't you have anyone?

I place another foot in the water. Cold cold cold and then not cold, merely smooth. Slimy reeds stroke my calves.

I did have family. But I was scared. Scared and shamed. They couldn't help me. He once threatened Maisie, my sister.

He'd kill her too, that's what he said. He'd blow her brains out and then his own. I believed him.

But to leave those boys? Those lovely boys? Mick and Jon – surely you couldn't leave your two lovely boys . . .?

I was tired, Rita. I just – couldn't think straight. You have to remember. Ten years of it, it wears you down. I loved Michael. I never loved anybody like I loved him and I just kept hoping if I loved him enough it would get better and it never did and the boys had seen so much already, I'd ruined their lives already. What use was I to them?

Cold water up to my waist now. I'm pushing out to the middle. A dragonfly buzzes around my stomach, the sun falls on my breasts in pools of white light. I trail my hands and they turn yellow in the green water, like flowers, trailing plants.

But they needed you. You left them with Michael. Look what's happened to them. Look at Mick.

But look at Jon. Mick has choices too, you know. Anyhow. There was nothing I could do. Nothing. I had no money. Michael controlled everything. I had no friends, he was so jealous, he never let anyone come to the house. I didn't work since I don't know when. Leaving takes energy. Everyone finds leaving hard, Rita. But I – was just – so – tired.

Tired. She sounds it. A little plop as I set out into the water. A cold splash at my face, arms stretching out in front of me, my heart pumping. The lily roots fall away from my legs. Taste of soil in my mouth.

I swim out towards the circle of dead trees. I want to see it up close. I push myself, swimming harder, my legs bunching up behind me like frog's legs. I'm surprised at my own speed. How breathless I am. And when I turn back, Frances in the buggy is just a tiny dot, with a red T-shirt lid.

Treading water, I'm trying to catch my breath.

I'm far far out and I can turn around in this lake and see trees all around me, it's like being at the bottom of a long tall glass of something. Something heady, intoxicating.

Tired. I'm tired too. My legs are aching, and it's a long swim back. The sun is burning the top of my head and I have an urge to put it under the water, to have my head as cool as my body.

It's no big deal. After all, it's just about giving up, isn't it? Giving in. Relaxing. Letting go. Trusting that something else – someone else – will hold me, take care of me, cradle me. Something I've wanted since I was tiny. To abandon myself to someone else. Or perhaps just to abandon myself.

No need to struggle, she says, softly. You've been fighting all your life, Rita, fighting to be seen, to be heard; why don't you admit defeat? You can't solve a thing, you can't change Mick and you can't escape him either, you can't ever escape how you feel about him. This is always going to hurt, just the way it does now: always, always. The only way you're going to escape is the way I did.

Be brave, Rita. Few people admit it, that they want out completely. It's religious. I been to enough of those church meetings to know that. Trust in God. Abandon yourself. Give up.

I let the water close over my face. I keep my eyes open and feel the circle coming smaller and smaller. I let my body go limp, but I still feel buoyant. The inside of my nose is burning. It's not that easy.

My foot brushes something and startled, despite my best intentions, I crash to the surface. I come noisily, spitting water, shaking wet hair, blowing like a sperm whale. What the fuck was that? What touched me? Bloody hell, what's under there?

Swimming as a kid, Dan would do it. Grab my leg under the water. Terrify me. Kicking, panicking, swallowing water, screeching and choking all at once, reaching for him, trying to smack him, punch him, scratch him, anything. That fury. At eight years old I wasn't afraid of it. I wanted to kill him.

Your foot touched a tree, I tell myself. A calm voice in

my head now, the soothing one I use with Frances. Don't panic. A frog, a fish. There's nothing in here to hurt you, no sharks or skinny wet brothers in swimming trunks. No one wanting to drag you down with them. It's only deep water and you'd better admit that you're frightened and the best thing to do is get out of it.

My heart thumping. The water like treacle. Frances is a long way off but I swim back towards her, arms and legs dragging, parting the water more and more slowly. I'm gasping and dizzy with the lack of breath, with the feeling of bursting in my lungs, with weariness. A hawk makes a shadow over the lake in front of me. My hand cuts the shadow. My head follows.

As I swim closer to the reedy bit, to the water's edge, I can see a man, sitting next to the buggy. I know without being able to make him out who it must be. Who else would come without a truck, silently? Who'd sit like that beside the baby, watching me? Someone tall and slim with brown hair and a khaki bag beside him.

# 25

When the water is up to my shoulders I call to Ryan.

'Hello! Ryan! Can you bring me my towel? It's on the grass, next to the buggy.'

I know he knows I'm naked. My clothes are in a heap on the towel, underwear too. He carefully shakes them off, walks up to the deep red soil at the water's edge, grinning and holding the towel in front of him.

I'm just going to have to brazen it out. It's a question of which is easiest, and pretending not to be embarrassed is easier than letting on that I am.

Ryan gives a low whistle and then pretends to cover his eyes as I wade clumsily out of the water, which seems to take a ridiculously long time, and there is nowhere else to look but straight at him, at his skinny legs in the faded black jeans, at his T-shirt with writing on it. And at his face with the Clint-Eastwood creases and the cigarette held between the teeth.

He holds the towel out for me with a playful show of gallantry and I can't help grinning too, as he wraps it around me. His watch brushes my arm; hot metal on my goose-pimpled skin. The sun is already warming me.

'Hi there, Rita,' he says and for a moment I think he's about to kiss me. Instead he takes the cigarette from his mouth and grinds it under his boot, then turns his back on me. Strides back to the buggy.

'Want these?' he says, offering me my glasses – a kind of reference to last time we met. I shake my head and he places them back on top of my T-shirt. Frances is still sleeping. Maybe I wasn't gone that long. I glance back over the lake and the water has closed up as if nothing ever touched it. The hawk circles now above the highest pine trees, over the other side. The lake has no interest in me, in my thoughts, in my wild dreams. Of course, of course.

I knot the towel securely under my arms and rearrange the T-shirt canopy to make sure Frances's head is covered. Then I sit down next to Ryan.

He is releasing a beer from the plastic rings of a six-pack and offers me one, which I accept.

'Enjoy your swim?'

I nod.

'How d'you get the bruises?'

I take a sip of beer. His question is so direct, it surprises me. And he isn't smiling, but looking straight at me. It feels like a challenge and maybe a challenge is the one thing that can make me tell.

'Mick. My boyfriend. We had a – bad – argument.'

'Some argument. What did he do?' He is cupping his hand around his mouth, lighting another cigarette.

'To tell you the truth' – I say this briskly, flatly, because there's no other way to say it – 'I don't really know. I was unconscious. I fell against a rock.' I stroke the place in my wet hair where the lump was, but can't seem to find it.

Ryan's face registers nothing. Not compassion, not shock, nothing prurient. Reassured, I carry on.

'Mick has a foul temper. It's so sudden. I've always known it about him but I thought it would be better out here. Instead it seems to be getting worse.'

I swig the beer, drinking it quickly, feeling it swill around in an empty stomach.

'Does he knock the kid around? Your baby?'

I hesitate. My first impulse is to say no, to be horrified. But it is the matter-of-fact way Ryan asks. As if he would expect that Mick would.

I let out a long sigh, I feel myself sinking.

'Well, not exactly. He frightens her. He does things that – might hurt her. He doesn't seem in control, and then sometimes I lose my temper and she – just gets caught in the middle.' I glance over at Frances, to avoid looking at Ryan. All I can see of her is the chubby little legs, healthy as two plump ears of sweetcorn.

Ryan inhales on the cigarette and blows out a twist of smoke.

'You about to leave him?'

'I don't know. I don't know what to do.'

Tears are hammering at the back of my head. I don't want to cry in front of Ryan, so I swallow hard, carry on talking.

'It's such a lot to give up. When we first came out here, I didn't know what to expect. Mick said he'd bought this land in North-East Washington, no electricity, no water . . . my friends thought I was mad. But in a weird kind of way, here isn't really that different from where I was, except that it is better.'

I gesture at the land, the sky, the lake, trying to think of a way to make Ryan see how this wilderness is like Dalston, London, struggle on, explaining.

'I mean, I love it. When I wake up in the morning and there's space and no sound of cars and we're far away from anywhere and there's only a chipmunk or a bird sound . . . But our life here. It's the same. We're hidden away, invisible. Just like we were in London. The people we hang out with – Jim, Nancy, you, this guy Buster that Mick's met – they're all . . .'

I don't know how to say this without insulting Ryan, but he is listening, pulling the ring-tab off another can of beer and then offering it to me.

'Well, you're all hoping. Just the way we are. Mick's into gold panning, he and Jim are going to Omak to get some dynamite so they can blast a few of the bigger rocks on our land. I mean, in London, that's all they ever did, sit around in squats, drinking tea and signing on the dole and making plans, adventures and trips and waiting for it all to magically come right . . .'

'And it hasn't, right? Now you're here – the great West hasn't lived up to your expectations?'

'No, that's just it. It has. The place has. The place is lovelier than I could have imagined. It makes me see how little I had in London, how little I have to go back to. I gave up a course I was doing, I packed up most of my stuff to send it out here. No home. No money. No job.'

He laughs, finishes his cigarette, placing the butt inside an empty beer can.

'Hey, who does? I lost my job, remember. And these fucking environmentalists are making sure I don't find no other kind—'

He points to the back of his T-shirt, then, when I appear not to click, offers me my glasses. The front has a recipe for spotted owl soup. Now I get it. A loggers' T-shirt. He represents everything Mick hates. A redneck. A logger. A member of the National Rifle Association. He's probably Pro-Life and believes in the death penalty, thinks that bitch in *Fatal Attraction* got what she deserved. Everything Mick hates. Isn't it everything I hate, too? In London it would be. In London I wouldn't even talk to him. But this isn't London. That's the point.

As if he's read my mind, Ryan says, 'Take a look at this,' and reaches in his back pocket, unfolds a map. Okanogan National Forest Travel Plan. I think he is going to show me where we are, point out the lake or something but instead he puts one brown, nicotine-stained finger on the lines about poachers. Poachers

Can Turn A Quick Profit So Can The People Who Turn Them In.

He reads it to me: 'Poaching is a well organised extremely lucrative practice. It's also a crime. One you can stop by calling the Washington Department of Wildlife and reporting any incident you may have witnessed. Earn up to $600 on violations involving moose, antelope, elk and endangered species; $500 for deer . . . there you go. Earn yourself a buck Rita. Phone the Poaching Hotline. There's your air-fare back to England.'

My mouth must have dropped open.

'What – turn you in? Do you really think I would?'

'I know you don't approve of me. I know that much.'

'But, well, yes, maybe I don't, but—'

'I'm just giving you some options, Rita. There are always options, I'm showing you that. There are good options and bad options, but there are options. It's just we don't always choose to take them . . .'

'I – you've got me wrong. I wouldn't turn you in. I'm – not – like that . . .'

'Don't look so shocked.' He's smiling at me again, his green eyes with those creases running right up into his hairline. He inhales on his cigarette, turns towards the lake. 'I'm trying to help you. I can see you're hurting. You don't have your friends, any family out here. I thought I'd point out a few things.'

'But I don't understand. Why show me that poaching hot-line? Why put yourself at risk?'

He finishes his can of beer and opens the last. Frances makes a little squeaking noise and her head lolls over to the other side in the buggy.

Ryan stretches out his legs, leans back on his elbows, drops his head back and closes his eyes. 'I know you won't turn me in,' he says softly. 'I know you like me.'

I could say to him: you cheeky bastard. He might just as

well have said: I know you want it. The beer is making me giddy. There is something in Ryan's confidence that reminds me of Mick. Of how I felt about Mick, early on. That challenge of a man who thinks he's God's gift. A man who loves himself, how exhilarating that is. Except of course it always turns out they never do.

I take a final drink of beer, drain the can. My head swims. The place above my eyes aches and when I roll over on my side beside Ryan I feel that my head is inside a woolly bag and my mouth is watering and the idea that just popped into my mind is the most normal one in the world.

It's something I get bored of. It's something Mick is always asking me to do, but I have to be in the right mood. Now, suddenly, Ryan is lying with his eyes closed and his arms folded behind his head and the sun is way way above him and his feet in their boots are crossed at the bottom and he is not asking anything of me, not telling me what he wants, what to do, not placing his hand over mine and demanding, the way Mick does.

I put my hand on his belt buckle, where the light bounces off it like a flame, and I'm watching his face.

His eyes are closed but it's as if something flew over his face. A butterfly. A shadow.

I undo the buttons, peeling the denim carefully open. I pause. I am scared. There's no doubt about it, I'm scared, but that's never bothered me before. I was scared the first time with Mick too. Three curls of light hair on his tanned stomach. A ridge already forming in his shorts that stirs as I brush my face on his stomach.

'Oh Ryan, you're so ... You're so sweet,' I murmur to him, my voice coming out slurred and beery. Things I can never say to Mick. Sweet. What's sweet? My heart jumping. The towel falls undone.

'Ryan,' I say, wetting my lips with my tongue. Feeling him

sigh and his erection grow again, his hand land in my hair, warm and sunny.

My chin brushes the buckle of his jeans. Smell of denim and familiar maleness and of clean cotton. Someone washes those shorts for him, maybe even irons them. A wife. I'm forming this thought even as I open my mouth around him, feel him on the roof of my mouth and hold him there, rubbing.

Now I have forgotten him and discovered something else. The comfort of sucking. The routine and rhythm of it. I could lose myself up here, lie in the sun all day, sucking. I know I am driving him demented, he needs to turn over and kneel up, wants me to do that worship bit, suck and lick and kiss and praise him, all over his stomach, rough him with my hair, but I'm just interested in sucking like a baby. My mouth has grown sensitive, my lips feel swollen and my body aches with a drunken joy, with longing.

I want to feel him come so I carry on, I want to be loving to him, as loving as I ever know how to be, I want to love someone with all my body and being and effort and to keep him, I want him to stay here in this place with me, this place in the lap of the mountain with trees all around us and ravens flying above us, in this bowl of desire but not over the other side, still stranded out here in the middle of deep water, of nowhere. I want Ryan because Ryan is kind to me, Ryan doesn't ask anything of me, Ryan will never hurt me, Ryan is beautiful and sweet . . .

But when he comes all I feel is disappointment. I'm tipped out of the bowl, of the spell, and what I'm left with isn't magic, or alchemy, or gold, or love, but something else. The messy stuff: tadpoles, DNA, whatever. The thing itself. How I got here in the first place.

Oh, Ryan. I roll over, away from him. He hasn't said a word. It occurs to me for the first time that he might be surprised. He's lying on his back, limp and wet and feeling for his cigarettes in his back pocket. I crawl up his body and kiss him on the mouth. He tastes of beer and of the lake. My face is soaking wet, I don't even know if I'm crying.

## 26

'Ryan, have you ever hit anyone?'

'Huh?'

'Have you ever hit someone? In anger. I just need to know.'

He's smoking of course, sitting up, his jeans buttoned up and his back and shoulders to me. He turns towards me to reply.

'Sure. I hit Jim Shaughnessy recently. Bust his truck, too.'

Somehow this registers in a way it shouldn't. I feel I know something of this story, before he tells it, and then remember why. My throat – a moment ago, warm, open, tries to close around the question I'm dreading asking.

'Ryan – is your name, I mean, do people call you – Smokey?'

He turns fully towards me, rolling over onto his stomach, but he doesn't seem surprised that I know.

'You heard. I guess everyone on the whole fucking mountain knows about Jim and Elly.'

But that isn't the story I know.

'I think we're talking about different things. Jim told us – it was when we first moved in – he showed us his truck where "Smokey" – you – had put a rock to it and he said . . .'

I'm fighting back panic, a spiralling sense of doom. 'He said Smokey was beating up on his old lady.'

Ryan makes an odd noise, a kind of snort and a choked bitter laugh, and it all comes out odd, like no sound I've ever heard.

'That fucking bastard. I wondered what he told his wife. How he explained his missing teeth.'

'So you mean —' I start. Again the words won't form.

*Please let it be true. Please don't let me be wanting to believe this so much that I don't know truth from lies.*

Ryan takes the cigarette from between his teeth, grinds it into the earth. He strokes my face with his finger, drops his eyes until I see nothing but the long eyelashes.

'I'm sorry, Rita. I guess I should have told you about Elly ...' He looks straight at me, half smiles, his hand unconsciously falls to his belt. 'But you know, you kinda took me by surprise ...'

'Oh I knew you were married,' I say hastily. 'I can always tell.' Bravado. Then more thoughtfully, I carry on: 'The married bit worries me less. I mean, I'm with Mick, aren't I? It's the thought – I mean for a moment, when I discovered you were Smokey, I thought: oh no, I've done it again. Picked a wife-batterer.'

'What, you picked one last time? You knew Mick was a wife-batterer?'

'No – of course not. But what I'm talking about – I mean, those theories. That some women must – subconsciously – want to be treated badly, like they have low self-esteem or they are secret masochists and attract violence to themselves, or something weird like that.'

'Do you believe that stuff?'

'I don't know. There must be a lot of women with low self-esteem if that's the case! To explain all the wife-battering, I mean.'

Ryan leans on his elbows, holding his chin. He draws on the cigarette.

'He ever hit you before you came out here?'

'No.' The reply is too quick. There is something. I don't know what it is about Ryan. Despite everything, I keep having this urge to trust him.

'Well. There was always his temper.' I glance sideways at Ryan, lie on my stomach too, cradle my chin in my hands. 'There was this one time – in the squat. I – I'd forgotten about it. Frances was about six months old. We were having a row, a silly row, I don't even know what it was about. Mick pushed me. That's all. But it was so hard – I fell against the gas fire. I hit my head. A little cut. Frances saw the blood. She was so young. But I remember her crying, her expression.'

My fingers rest on my mouth. I'm staring at the lake and the ring of skeleton trees in its centre. A sigh escapes through my fingers. Ryan is silent. It's his lack of comment, of judgement. I don't know what it is, this feeling – perhaps gratitude, maybe it's just horniness. Or longing, this overwhelming longing to give up, to trust *somebody*. The trees float together in a grey blur. Tears are hammering at my temples again.

'Mick was really – sorry. It was just a push, it didn't really hurt me. I – I suppose I just put it to the back of my mind. I was doing this course. Studying psychotherapy. I thought I could rescue people, I wanted to sort people's lives out for them. But I can see I don't know anything, I know fuck all.'

Ryan's eyes narrow against the smoke. He swats at a mosquito about to land on my hand.

'I'm no wife-batterer.' In his pupils I can see the trees reflected. 'My wife is sleeping with Jim Shaughnessy. I've known for about a year. One time I caught them together in Jim's truck and I lost it. That's the one and only time I ever hit someone.'

'OK.' A pause. 'I'm sorry. I believe you.'

'Much fucking good it did me, anyhow.'

'She didn't end the affair?'

'Who knows? I can't tell what Elly's up to any longer. I only know she doesn't want me.'

He blows the remark away from me, floats it on the smoke.

Frances makes a little grunting sound, and we both glance over at the buggy. She's been asleep for about four hours, one of her record naps, which I know I'll pay for later; she'll be awake half the night.

Aware that our conversation is about to be interrupted, Ryan suddenly turns to me, gently lifts the hair away from my face, kisses my nose. 'I don't know any of that therapy stuff. But it seems to me your situation is like mine. You fell in love with someone. That person turned out different from how you imagined. Now you have to figure out what you want, what to do. And leaving is tough, for anyone. It's a whole fuck of a lot harder when you're shit-scared and worn out, the way you are.'

I roll onto my back on the towel, staring at the sky, watching the sun grow bigger, turn into a huge blob of gold and then shoot away again, become tiny and sun-sized. I'm so grateful to Ryan that desire wells up again, my body is flooded with heat from head to toe.

Frances has opened her eyes. Ryan hands me my glasses, my shorts, the T-shirt from the top of the buggy, and helps to put it on over my head. He readjusts his belt, grins, kisses me on the mouth. I glance at Frances.

'You shouldn't drink in this heat on an empty stomach. I was thinking you must be nauseous,' he whispers. 'Here, drink this.'

From the khaki bag he hands me a bottle of water. The liquid is warm and when I open my mouth to drink, my jaw makes clicking sounds in my ears.

Frances is stirring and forming a cry, her face red and screwed up, shiny and overheated.

'This is Ryan. Mummy's friend. Or do you prefer to be called Smokey?'

'Ryan is fine.'

'Wy-an. Mummy's fwend,' says Frances. Too late I think, God help me if she repeats it. That's the balance – always weighing up Frances's well-being against mine. If I don't introduce Ryan, how can she trust me, how can she feel safe if one day she wakes up and there is a strange man around and no explanation?

Ryan strides off to pee in the bushes, comes back whistling, swinging the bag over his arm. His mood has shifted and he keeps grinning at me, he looks about fifteen, like a schoolboy who just stole his first CD. I put my glasses on, staring at him. The cat who got the cream.

We start walking, me pushing the buggy, Ryan lighting up, down towards the road. Frances suddenly yells 'Sindy! Sindy!' and I have to run back and get her doll, finding it lying face down, the bare plastic bum sticking up in the air in a posture of defiance and vulnerability. Frances must have flung her into the trees just before she fell asleep.

'You gonna be OK?' Ryan asks. I'm walking in exaggerated slowness, stopping every time the buggy hits a pine cone, without the energy needed to manoeuvre Frances over it.

'I don't want to go back,' I say. The words drop out like stones. I feel sick.

'We could walk a little. Go to my place.'

'You live round here?'

'I have a shack near Lone Star track. Near the Wishing Stone. It was Bob – my Dad's – he's gone now. I live in Goldtown.'

'With your wife,' I say.

'With my wife.'

We walk on in silence.

'No I better go back.' Now I'm sober and angry.

He accepts this mildly, standing still while I wheel the buggy around, change direction.

'Meet me tomorrow.' he says. 'At the Wishing Stone. Midday. Mick's gonna be apple-picking, right?'

I pause. I stare at the dust tracks on the wheels of the buggy. The road is white, dusty, rocky. Between a rock and a hard place. Dalston, Mount Coyote, what does it matter? I don't know what the fuck to say, what to do. I don't know anything, anything at all.

'Why don't you apple-pick, if you're out of work?' I ask, at last, for something to say.

'What do you think? Jim works there, right?'

'Of course. Sorry.'

Ryan puts his hand on my hair, strokes a strand away from my face, gently pulling it from under the arm of my glasses.

'Rita, you're gorgeous, you know that?' he says it softly, his face in my hair. I'm staring at Frances, at the top of her head. Gorgeous. Am I? I make a move to start walking again, to push the buggy, but Ryan turns me around to face him.

'And you're adventurous too. I can see that. You have courage.'

'Do I? Do you really think so?'

'You're out here aren't you? Just look at yourself.' A quick grin again. I notice nicotine stains on his teeth, and for no reason I can think of, the ugly stains comfort me.

'Shall I see you tomorrow, Rita? Midday. The Wishing Stone. Leave the baby.'

A kiss on the cheek. His skin is like sandpaper. I watch him walk up the road, like a scene in a film, the closing or opening credits, I can't decide which; the lone mountain road, the tall thin stranger in dazzling sun-light, kicking a stone, bag over his shoulder.

*Ryan's bag has a gun in it. I'm starving. My head is aching, my jaw is aching; all of me is aching. Who the hell can I leave Frances with?*

\* \* \*

Mick gets back all excited and full of presents; a huge brown bag of Washington Reds, some letters for me from the box in Goldtown, six bottles of Bud, a local newspaper with news of the latest gold find in Chesaw.

I decline the Bud, my head still throbbing, and open the *Okanogan Valley News* to read about the gold mine.

New Poll Shows Majority Favour Gold Mine. Goldtown – a new telephone poll, commissioned by Black Ruby Gold Company indicates that as many as 95 per cent of those with an opinion, feel that a proposed mine near Chesaw would be a 'good idea'.

'Well, what dickhead wouldn't think it was a good idea?' Mick is stripping off to wash with a bowl of washing-up water, on the deck. I'm frying pork chops on the barrel-stove, talking to him through the open door. Frances is on the deck with Mick, watching a humming bird buzzing like a tiny motorbike, hovering at the few remaining fuchsias wilting in the early evening heat.

'Houston-based Black Ruby Gold Company, predicted that the company could start mining as early as 1992,' I read, 'provided that there are no legal appeals. The draft Environmental Impact Statement for the proposed ninety-acre – God Mick, ninety acres, did you read that? – open-pit gold mine is currently at the printers.'

'Yeah, Jesus, ninety acres!' Mick yells, coming into the cabin and setting the bowl down on the floor with a splash, drying under his arms with his T-shirt.

'This is it, Rita, I'm sure of it. If there's gold at Chesaw, and that much of it, there's gold here too, you can bet. Jim says to keep quiet about it. We'd just need to blast some out, then take it over the border to Canada and do a deal for it.'

'What's this EIS they keep going on about in this article?' I ask him.

'It's on Okanogan National Forest Land. It's going to make

one hell of a fuck-up. They have to do an environmental survey, all that kind of stuff. Legal stuff.'

'Will it make a mess of our place? When you and Jim start blasting?'

'Sure. But not on that scale. We only need a little bitty bit of gold to make money, honey . . .'

I finish reading the paper while the chops are sizzling. Dr Richards Answers Your Questions. Sponsored by the Goldtown Free Methodist Church. *Let me speak plainly to the homemaker with a busy, non-communicative husband: You cannot depend on this man to satisfy all your needs.* Dr Richards goes on to suggest exercise classes, church activities, bicycle clubs, whatever.

After tea, I remember about the letters. I read them by lamplight, the fire is snapping, Frances, well rested after her long nap is wide awake and pestering Mick, poking little fat fingers and then the Sindy doll up the leg of his shorts as he dozes in the chair. This is such a sexual gesture that I panic for a moment.

'Frances, don't do that. Leave Daddy alone. Here, have a piece of apple.'

I slice her a piece of the red apple I'm eating and she settles on the dusty floor, contentedly pushing her piece of apple through the cracks between the two by fours.

I read the letter from England first. It's from my Mum.

Dear Rita,

Hope this letter finds you well. Things are well with us. Pam had her baby – a little boy, 8 pounds, Tony is well pleased, even caught him changing a nappy once. Can you believe that!

Glad to hear things are good out there, and that the cabin is shaping up. Nighttimes sound a bit bloody scary – you must worry about bears and things? You always were scared of the dark. I don't know how you manage. Mind you, not as bad as Tony. Scared of his own shadow. What a worry that boy was. You should see him now, Rita. What a Dad. I'm well proud of him, seriously I am.

Sorry this is so short. I must get off now and catch the post. Give little Frances a kiss from me. Watch her skin now, in that heat. We all miss you.

Love, Mum

It's the longest letter I've ever had from her. I dutifully give Frances a kiss on the cheek, while she swats at me with the palm of her hand.

We both start as a grey deer-mouse runs along a log under the window and disappears behind the sawdust fringes of the velvet curtain in the bathroom. Frances runs to find it.

I open the second letter, which is from Carole. It too is very short. Carole's handwriting is just as I'd expect, big, carefully formed letters, slightly teenage, somehow, with a fancy curl on all the ys and gs.

Thursday

Rita,

Thought you could use this. Don't tell Mick. There's no need to pay me back.

Carole

Inside the note is a money order for 600 dollars.

## 27

Mum always worries about Tony most. Even now. Even though I'm the youngest. The year Dad leaves, we move. It isn't far away, we still go to the same school, in fact now we are nearer to it. Mum says the council has transferred us, it wasn't right, me and Tony having to share a room and Tony nearly a teenager now.

So now we aren't on the sixth floor, and we have a low wall at the front of the house which is great to hide behind and jump out at people as they are walking past in the street. And we have a street and a number instead of a name for our block of flats and there is a tree in a square box of earth in the pavement outside, with a long name something like Staghorn Sumach. I make a drawing of it in a book and sit up it all day long while Sindy and Action Man lie entangled under some camouflage netting on the concrete below.

But the new bedroom is lonely and I can't sleep at night because I miss hearing Tony snuffling and talking in his sleep and the bed-springs creaking as he turns over, and without those Donny Osmond stickers on the wall next to my cheek. We don't have curtains yet and sometimes the moon looks right in at the window and we never hear the pigeons cooing any more or people kicking milk-bottles over and of course the ghost of Dad doesn't come to this new house – I don't know if Dad even knows we're here yet, because he hasn't visited us and if I ask Mum about it she just tuts and tells me to set the table or fetch her the scissors.

So I go in Mum's big bed, and she grumbles and moves over to let me in and I lie in the warm bit where her body was and it smells of her perfume and her washing powder and her shampoo. Her long straight hair spreads out all over the pillow like a huge spider.

'Mum, I need the lamp on.'

'Rita, get to sleep. It's four o'clock in the morning.'

'Mum, I'm scared. Can I put the light on?'

'NO!'

Then I'm sniffling and trying not to let her hear me cry but the big lump of her turns over and her thin arm comes out and her voice is softer and her face turns to me in the dark.

'What is it love? You never used to be scared of the dark.'

More snuffling and crying. Her hand starts stroking my hair, pulling a wet strand away from my mouth. She has a pale nightdress on with long sleeves and the cuff brushes my cheek. Her thin nose sticks out like a little rock in a dark pool and I touch it with my finger. It feels icy.

'Mum. How old are you?'

'Thirty-six. Why?'

'Is that old?'

'No. Not really.'

She turns to lie on her back. She scratches her throat and she is staring up at the ceiling. I see her long curved throat and it is like a swan's neck. She is so lovely.

'Mum . . . when will you die?'

She turns back to face me. I thought she would answer me straight away, tell me not to be silly or something, not to worry about that, to go to sleep and forget such silly things but instead she is staring at me really hard. Even in the dark I can see her swallow. I feel her warm coffee-breath when she speaks.

'Oh Rita. I don't know. Nobody knows. And that's the truth.'

'But will it be soon?' Tears in my voice again. 'It won't be soon, will it? Because then we won't have anyone because Dad's gone and who will make the dinner and we'll all starve . . .'

Again I'm thinking she will laugh and ruffle my hair and call me her silly girl and say 'is that all I'm good for, to make the dinners?' but she isn't laughing and her face looks tired. I'm frightened of that face, she does look old, perhaps she really will die soon and now she doesn't look like Mum at all, she looks like a witch, so old, and ugly; dark and full of shadows. This scary feeling, it was just behind her, waiting in a deep, tight ball. Now it has rolled right into her face.

A long sigh. Nasty coffee-smelling sigh.

'I don't know if it will be soon, Rita. I hope not. I suppose not. I don't suppose I'm going to die for a very long time. So I will be here to cook your dinners until you're easily big enough to cook them yourselves. OK?'

I'm lying there and staring at her and listening and it's horrible the way she says it and the ball, the tightly wound ball of something, of string, of trouble, is unravelling and wrapping itself right around my heart and it's in my chest now, pulling tight, tighter. I feel like I can't breathe.

*Stay and cook our dinners. Stay.*

'Go to sleep now, and don't worry.'

The tired voice again. She turns over, her back to me.

The bed creaks and the tickly edges of the candlewick stroke my face as I turn towards her, put my face close, but not touching, her shoulders in the pale yellow nightdress.

*My Dad's gone and he's never coming back.*

Jon, being younger, can cry, and he does. He cries in the evenings when the strange Auntie comes to stay and can't find the pyjamas with the red stripes on, or remember that he isn't allowed Cheerios last thing at night; he cries when he is dropped at the new school in Mount Vernon where the teacher keeps calling him Jim by mistake and has told the children never to mention his Mommy, so that they all do, every break time, asking over and over, 'What happened to your Mom?'

Mick hovers around his brother. He has no desire to make friends, in class he stares at the scratchings on the wooden desk in front of him; in break, he hangs around Jon, ready to put his arm around his brother whenever he cries, and to punch the child who provoked it. This is how he gets his reputation – tough, mean, a bully; even the kindest teacher, even the sweet Miss Wilson whose home is full of stray cats and birds with broken wings, finds it hard to remember that Mick is only a child when he gets into one of his rages; glowing with fury, launching into a stream of obscenities.

When Mick stabs Gary Henderson with his compass, Michael Senior is called up to the school. He has to squirm on the brown draylon sofa in the headmaster's office, while being told all Mick's misdemeanours to date. He takes his embarrassment out on Mick the second he gets hold of him, which (fortunately for Mick) is in the school playground; meaning that a member of staff has to call the police to remove Michael Senior from the school premises. Mick, arms by his sides, watches as his father is escorted, shouting, through the school gates, and knows what's in store for him at home.

Jon cries every night in his sleep, sometimes waking himself or Mick with dry, noisy sobs. When this happens, Mick goes to get the furry raccoon, slipping it onto the pillow in front of his brother's face, and says 'sssh, wake up, you're dreaming, here's raccoon,' and usually that does the trick, Jon will doze back again. Now it's Mick who's wide awake, and for him, falling back to sleep is impossible. In the next room, Michael is sleeping, an unshaven, unwashed mess, usually drunk, and these days the three of them are held together by Aunt Maisie, who has moved in and sleeps in a rose-patterned heap on the living-room sofa, under one of Cherie-Rose's old quilts.

When Mick wakes like this, the entire house at Mount Vernon is cloaked in something, something so dense, so cloying, it seeps in through his mouth, hits the back of his throat, lies heavy in the pit of his stomach. He has to battle through a smog to get from room to room; grief hangs in the air like a muggy cloud and there is always, somewhere, the scent of Cherie-Rose, a smell which only Mick knows; his version of his mother, nobody else's. He doesn't know how much he misses her, because he doesn't realise how much he loved her. He is angry with her. Jon was her favourite and Jon didn't need to be – he has Mick to take care of him. Mick, at eleven years old, feels like an old man, tired, unloved and bitter.

Mick cries once, and only once, about the loss of his mother. It's when Aunt Maisie presses 2 dollars in his hand, telling him to buy himself something nice. His first instinct is to put it in his saving book, to feel a little pang close to pleasure, a sensation he hasn't felt in so long that it is an instant, strong sensation, like a prick from a needle. Then he remembers what he had been saving for, and bursts into tears. There is a gold handbag in Woolworth's in Waukesha that he knows Cherie-Rose will love. And with that thought comes a tide of others; how much he understood, really; how unhappy he knew she was, how painfully he had wanted to make everything right, protect her, make her feel better. If only, Mick is thinking, at eleven years old, I'd finished saving up and bought her the handbag. The gold handbag. I could have saved her. She'd still be here.

The deep anger inside him is something precious, something she gave him and he doesn't know that the reason he treasures it, polishes it, keeps it bright and fresh, is because it is the only expression of his grief, his last connection to Cherie-Rose, to his mother.

I have the best analysed batterer around. Finally, surely, I've done it, I've done what women long to do: I've worked him out. Lying in bed beside Mick, trying to shift position without disturbing or touching him, a wave of sadness creeps up my body, stealing up from my toes. So what? a little voice goes. *So what?*

When I wake Mick has already left. I turn over in the lumpy bed and a mosquito is buzzing in my ear. I remember Ryan and my stomach rumbles emptily. My veins feel full of petrol. The cabin is in bright, white sunlight. I lie on my back, blinking. The more I lie there, the whiter the light seems to be. It suddenly occurs to me that it is a strange kind of light, it is fluttering, it is moving, buzzing.

I lean on one elbow to look out of the little square window next to the bed. At first I think there is a snow storm. Then I realise that what we are in is a storm of butterflies. We're inside one of those tumbling plastic scenes; Log Cabin in a Forest in a Snow Storm and someone just tipped it up and shook it about. What's happening? It's only August. I dress quickly, wake Frances.

'Futterfwies,' says Frances, stretching her hand to the window. We watch their jerky flight for a while. They cluster around the tops of the Ponderosas, in a frenzied whirling mass, like pieces of paper, unable to settle.

'Aren't they beautiful?' I say to Frances. 'Like snow. Pretty.'

'Pwetty,' she says.

I sit Frances on the bed to pull her socks on and change her nappy. Mostly now she doesn't wear one. But I am planning to take her to Nancy's so daren't risk an accident. Toilet training, all of that. If I was in Dalston now I'd be having conversations with other Mums, with the health visitor. At the mother and toddler class. The One O'clock club. It occurs to me for the very first time that Frances and I are missing out on something. But then I think: what's best for Frances – to be pushed around Clissold Park looking at a few poxy ducks through a wire mesh fence or to be here, watching a blizzard of butterflies in a wild mountain forest? I stick the tabs on the nappy, kiss her fat talcum powder belly, let her tangle her fingers in my hair.

'Going to see Nancy,' I tell her, strapping her into the stroller. I am thinking 'stroller' rather than buggy because I know that is what Nancy will call it. Outside the butterflies are beginning to disturb me, their constant movement is flickering on my glasses; it's like interference on a TV screen.

'Futterfwie, futterfwie!' sings Frances as I push her down the drive, jabbing Sindy's feet up towards the shiny blue-green tops of the trees.

The strange part is that by the time we get to Nancy's the butterflies are gone.

'Oh those,' says Nancy, pouring me a coffee and shooing the two biggest dogs out of the kitchen while I unstrap Frances and fold the stroller.

'Pine beetles. That's what you have. It's a kind of moth. Your trees are infested, you need Mick to cut those ones down or you gonna find all your trees have it.'

'It's a pest then?' I ask.

'It sure is. Sounds like you have it bad too. The beetle burrows into the bark earlier in the year – so you had a problem all this time – but you don't see any sign of it until late summer when they turn into moths . . .'

'Oh,' I mutter. 'They look so pretty.'

'Sure they're pretty,' Nancy says, pushing a strand of her auburn hair behind her ear and smoothing floury hands down her apron. 'But they're lethal.'

'Oh.'

She is wearing a sweatshirt although the temperature in her kitchen is making us both sweat. World's Greatest Mom. All three kids are outside; messing around on bikes, so I gather it must be the summer holiday. Nancy spoons lumps of biscuit dough onto a tray in white dollops, pauses to shout at Clay to find the bike for the baby, chatters on about Jim and Mick and when she pauses I finally manage to ask her.

'I just wondered. Nancy. Um, Frances has just been around me all the time. Since we got here. No other kids to play with. I mean, I know you have a lot on your plate already with three kids and I hate to ask this but it's just for today, but I wondered if you could have her for a few hours? I wanted to – go into Goldtown to the store and the laundromat and she hates it there—'

Bad excuse. Goldtown. She knows I haven't got the truck (but I don't know if she knows I can't drive) so how does she think I'll get there.

'You hitchin'?' she says, matter of fact, opening the door of the huge barrel-shaped oven to check the heat.

I seize on this. 'Yes. Is it safe, do you think?'

'Well, anybody you meet up here is likely to be local. Smokey. Buster. Old Fisher – someone like that. I suppose it's safe enough. But I wouldn't do it.'

'Oh.'

I twitch at the word 'Smokey', feeling the colour rise in my face. Now what can I say? I can hardly flout her sound advice and hitch regardless. Nancy puts the tray of biscuit mix in the oven, straightens up, sips her coffee.

'Do you need a break, Rita?'

Frances is outside now. I see her through the open door, straddling the trike that Clay has fetched for her, and smacking at him angrily as he tries to show her how to peddle it.

From the way she is looking at me I know Nancy is thinking of the time she saw me smack Frances. I don't want to remember this, I don't want Nancy to remember it and yet it is useful. She thinks I'm cracking up and asking for time away from the baby.

'I don't mind having her. Sure. That's fine, Rita. Anytime.'

'Oh, it's just for today, honest. That would be great.'

'No problem.'

'I – here's her juice and a spare – diaper – and she might need a nap just after lunch and . . .'

Nancy smiles at me. She is clearing blobs of dough from the bench where she is working, wiping with a cloth and some Envirofriendly something or other and I'm thinking: Bloody hell. *World's Greatest Mom. Jesus is My Lord.* Why doesn't she just wear a sweatshirt saying 'I'm perfect' and have done with it?

'More coffee?' she offers, holding out the pot. Her heart-shaped face is shining from the heat in the kitchen and now the smell of dough is beginning to rise, mixing with the smell of warm dogs and burning pine.

But I accept the coffee, squeezing myself behind the ladder to sit down on a dog-haired sofa in the adjoining room, the living-room I suppose you'd call it, if log cabins have living-rooms. There's no rush. Ryan said midday and even though I have half a dozen pine moths dancing in my stomach, I'm also glad suddenly of the normalness of Nancy's home. Coffee. Children. Dog-hairs.

'You know Jim's an alcoholic,' says Nancy, the minute I sit down.

'What?'

Her eyebrows are arched in two high crescent moons. I stare at these as she continues talking.

'I've tried to get him to A-Anon. There's one in Sinkalip. I've tried to introduce him to Jesus. But so far' – she rubs a little dough off her finger, makes a ball with it, goes to the door, drops it outside, comes back – 'no luck. But I'm praying for him.'

'Yes. Yes,' I say. Does she know about Jim and Elly? Does she, in fact, know everything?

Under those two crescent moons Nancy's eyes are wide and impossible to read. I'm wondering if there are rules. Am I supposed to disclose something now. Is it a trade? Jim's an alcoholic – Mick hits me. Why is it that I think everybody knows, really? That I have it written all over me. I am a Failure. I am a Bad Person. The person I love uses his fists on me. I take my glasses off, rub them on my T-shirt, playing for time. I'm thinking of Ryan's shiny buckle belt, and his long thin forearms with their weaving veins. Veins. I shouldn't have thought of them. The butterflies start up a drum beat.

'Um. Nancy. You have three lovely children. I love your kids. They are so – so like proper kids should be. You really are doing a great job.'

This comes out in a rush. It bewilders me. It isn't what I'd meant to say, but it's the truth, it's what I believe. To my horror her eyes soften into circles of light; she's about to cry.

She wipes them hastily with the back of her sleeve.

'I know, I know,' she murmurs, 'I love my kids. If it wasn't for them – Jim's a good man, you know, we've been here a long time now. Twelve years of my life here. I worry about Randy. I think it's hardest on him, being the eldest boy . . . One night Jim fell – we had a party you know – and he fell in the fire – it was dying but there was some heat still – and I was dragging Jim out, he was so heavy, you know, and I was calling to Randy, screaming to him, help me, help me get your father outa here – and that boy, he just stood there. He says he hates him. He hates me for staying with him. Oh Rita. I try. The Lord knows I try. But sometimes I think you just can't be a good Mom under certain conditions. No one can.'

Now I don't know if she is talking about me or her. I just know I want to escape. Something is happening to me, that

I wasn't expecting, it's as if I've come up out of water and shaken my head and suddenly my ears are popping and I can hear properly and a smeary veil is lifting, a film which covered everything, every encounter. Something is entering me but I want to keep it out, out, I want to run away from it. The note from Carole and the $600 money order is in the pocket of my shorts. Nancy is offering me coffee in her kitchen and baking biscuits and offering to take care of my baby for me, simply because I need her to. The forest is infested and the ducks at Clissold Park are beckoning.

I finish wiping my glasses and put them back on. Clay comes running in screeching that Frances rammed the bike at him and flourishing the cut. Nancy is soon immersed in a flurry of Band-aid and cold water and soothing noises. She sends them off with Marie-Lu biscuits and a kiss on the hurt places. She's right, I know, it's impossible to be a good enough mother, the mother you long to be, under certain conditions. I'm thinking of Cherie-Rose. Or Tina, my mother; in those first months after he left she must have been sleeping with my Dad, keeping it secret from us, because despite his promises, he didn't come and see us, couldn't be bothered with any of us. And I'm thinking now of Frances with that blood-red poppy splash on her mouth and her big, frightened eyes and the way she loves Mick best and she'll never snuggle on my lap the way she does on his. Why do we blame our mothers for everything, everything?

Nancy is standing at the open doorway of the cabin, looking at me. She holds her hand out for the empty coffee cup.

'Anytime you need to leave the baby with me. That's fine. I can see you're – kinda tired. You must miss your folks back in England, I guess.'

She's slipping her hands into a thick grey oven glove, pulling the tray of biscuits out of the oven. It's as if she never said a word about Jim. As if she unzipped a skin, stepped out of it, spoke, and then stepped back into it again. Now it is zipped up to the chin.

'Won't have to do this for much longer,' she comments, struggling with the heavy oven door and the plate of biscuits.

'How d'you mean?'

'Next year we're gettin' electricity. Jim's promised me an electric oven when we do . . .' I know I look startled, horrified even, but her back is to me, she carries on, 'The whole of Mount Coyote. You know the Lot Range, who own the mountain? They finally gave in. We'll have electric road lights, the works—'

'I – sort of – like the mountain without electric lights. The darkness. There aren't many places where you can see – have – real darkness, without any electricity for miles . . .' I'm trying to disguise the upset in my voice, it's illogical, it's absurd, but it's so final, the end of something.

'Well, it sure is inconvenient. All those lamps and candles. It's positively dangerous.'

I have to agree that it is. She holds out a warm biscuit – I would call it a scone, but whatever it is, despite how delicious, it is hot, and lumpen and perhaps too much for me; it refuses to be swallowed, so that I have to push it to one side in my mouth with my tongue so that I can say goodbye.

'Thanks a lot Nancy. I'll be back in the afternoon. I – hope she's no trouble for you.'

Still holding the rest of the biscuit, I step out into the dry air of the morning, fresh and hot after the smoky kitchen. I kiss Frances and pop the warm nugget of biscuit into her mouth, without Nancy seeing. I still have a lump in my throat. I don't know whether to burst into tears or swallow it.

I'm thinking about Ryan's hands, the square nails, surprisingly clean, the straight fingers, the smoky marks, index finger, right hand. How familiar those hands seem to me.

Even the bruise, the giant bruise on Ryan's upper arm, where the rifle butted against it, only seems to make Ryan more familiar; more like me. He has the most beautiful hands I ever saw on a man and thinking about them now is erasing the conversation with Nancy; making my blood leap, making all the little parts of me stand on end.

## 29

The Wishing Stone is a mile or so north of Top Lake, along Lone Star road. The trees thin out, I'm on a plateau now, on the top of Mount Coyote and the forest and the chokecherry and snowberry become sage-brush and grass. The stone is close to the road and when I reach it I can see Ryan's cabin, a few hundred yards away, set back in the fields. Mick and I have driven past it many times, this is the route to Goldtown – but today is the first time I've noticed smoke curling from the chimney.

Ryan is waiting by the stone, a small figure, seated with his knees up. Smoking, of course. Instantly the taste of him is back in my mouth and I can't look at his face, I have to swallow hard. The words *act normal* form in my mind and then I want to laugh. What the fuck is normal? I can't believe I'm here.

'I've always wanted to look at this,' I say, meaning the Wishing Stone. 'What is it?'

'That ain't it,' Ryan laughs. 'That's some plaque they put there to satisfy the Indians on the Colville reservation. The stone is long gone. Blasted by settlers looking for gold.' I feel foolish. Of course. The stone is too new, and going up to it now, brushing the long grasses that partially obscure the writing, I read:

The Wishing Stone or Camas-woman is one of many

wishing stations or shrines in the Northwest, where Indians made offerings. To pass Camas-woman without depositing a gift was said to bring sorrow and ill-luck. After the Indian's contact with the fur-traders, coin entered largely into the gifts, and the white men, learning of the Camas-woman's influence robbed her of all her wealth. When the Colville Reservation was thrown open to settlement in 1900, a prospector dynamited the shrine to see if it contained anything of value. Originally five feet in height, all that is left of the stone are the shattered parts found around this site.

'Anything of value. Gold. What a mess,' I say, looking around at the rubble, the odd beer can, the long grasses and fireweed. I don't know if it's the place, the conversation I just had with Nancy, or Ryan, or what. A huge wave of grief washes over me; everyone is sad. Ryan, waiting for his wife. Cherie-Rose, giving up. Mick, thrashing and struggling to come to the surface. Frances, bobbing helplessly, the whole fucking population of the Colville reservation; everyone.

Ryan says nothing, blows out smoke in hoops.

I stare at him for a long time. The fine hair of his eyebrows, a tiny piece of grass which has landed in his hair, the mouth shaping an o. Yes, he is certainly beautiful, in a fine, thin kind of way. He's a willowy Quaking Aspen to Mick's giant Engleman Spruce. This image lands in my mood with a small plop, dispersing it.

I sit down beside Ryan and to break the silence ask him, 'Do you know anything about Coyote? The Coyote stories in this area . . .'

'He talks out his ass.'

'What?'

'That's the story. When Coyote needs advice, he shits. The shits talk to him, tell him what to do. If he don't like what they tell him he threatens to rain on them, wash them away.'

I muse on this. It sounds plausible enough – it fits with the idea of Coyote being either foolish or clever, take your pick – but without the Mourning Dove book, how can I be sure? I could ask Ryan how he knows, but decide against it. Listen to your shit, let it advise you. Listen to the shit you're in.

'It doesn't look like anybody comes here,' I say.

'Why would they? It's smashed.'

'Oh, I don't know. To pay – what's it called? – homage. To wish for something . . .? Even just as a tourist attraction. It's like Old Holson. No one seems to go there either.'

I draw my knees up to my chest and we're like two garden gnomes, sitting there, gazes fixed. We aren't touching, there's around six inches between my thigh and his and this is the place – the grass and earth between us – that I concentrate on. I look down at the ground, fiddling with a stick of grass, drawing lines in the earth.

'Wish for something then. Why don't you?' Ryan says, tilting his body ever so slightly towards me. I know he wants to touch me by the way he is looking at me. I am suddenly ten years old and buying an ice-cream from a van. The old man holding my hand in his for just a moment too long when I give him the money. I don't know how I understand at ten years old the peculiar quality of those eyes, my feeling that it's wrong, wrong, the way he is looking at me, but I do. I shift slightly away from Ryan, concentrate on a tiny black beetle running on the ground, chase it with my little stick of grass.

'What would I wish for? I don't know. I don't know what I want.'

'Money? Love? Everlasting happiness?' Ryan suggests. His hand rests on my forearm, then on the hand circling with the stick. He closes his fingers around mine.

'Yeah. Any of those. All of those.' My voice is flat. I don't even sound sarcastic. The sadness is threatening again, closing in on me, and not even Ryan, perhaps especially not Ryan, can keep it at bay. What do I want? What would I wish for if I could have anything at all, but only one thing? An end to world hunger? Peace in Northern Ireland? Mick to love me for ever and ever?

He moves ever so slightly. The cigarette is finished, I know he is going to kiss me, and the light is gathering, fluttering and massing like moths. Instead of kissing me, Ryan removes my glasses, puts them gently on the ground beside the stone plaque. Then turns towards me and the moment where I am waiting for him to kiss me begins again.

'Rita.' His voice is very quiet. 'You know I like you a real lot.'

He strokes the hair away from my face with one hand. His face is close. I can see the flecks of yellow light in his green eyes.

I bite back the urge to say something glib, or to question him, and instead, I watch his eyes, say simply 'Yes.'

'And I – not – just – you know, in a sexual way . . .' and he is struggling, so I let him go on. 'I like you. I never met anybody like you before. Really, I mean it. The – the – way you talk. The things you say.'

'It's not just my lovely bottom, then?' This is out, before I can stop myself, I know I'm trying to fend him off with flippancy; anything to prevent this conversation, the one I know we're having, the painful, impossible one, about him and me.

He stares down at the ground between us, at the dry earth, the tiny sticks of burnt grass. An ant is running in circles in its own little forest of grass and pebbles and impossibile hurdles.

Ryan glances up finally, sighs.

'Don't get me wrong. I don't mean to – advise you. Hell, what do I know, about all that fucking stuff, about anything? But I just wanted to say that – I think you – you know, I know you're hurting already and I don't want to add to that. I love

Elly still, I have to tell you that. I don't know if it can work – but you, you deserve more, Rita. You deserve better.'

I sense that he's disappointed with himself, thinks the struggle was wasted, he hasn't managed to get the feelings across. But he's wrong. I lean forward to kiss him and when my mouth lands on his, I know we've had the conversation anyway.

I have to let go of something, leave it behind. It's simple, but it's potent, it's only this. No one is going to rescue me.

A wish is forming. A wish forms like a thread, a spider's web, as fine as silk. I have a wish. I make a wish.

When I arrive at Nancy's to pick up Frances I'm hurrying, plucking pieces of grass from my hair, my legs aching from the long walk back from Lone Star track. At the sight of me between the two big trees at the bottom of the drive the dogs come bounding over, and Nancy is following them, practically running. I know something is wrong. It takes me a moment to grasp why, what has set up this warning drum in me, then I realise. It's Nancy. She's wearing a different skirt. She has shoes on, instead of trainers. Her hair is brushed. And her freckled face, approaching me now, is paler than the moon.

'Rita! Hi! I've had some bad news . . .'

'Is it Frances? The baby, what, what?'

She looks distracted, seems to have trouble comprehending.

'No, no,' she mutters, clutching one of the dogs by the scruff of the neck, walking me back to the cabin. 'It's my Mom. She had an automobile accident. I just had the letter. I have to go visit her in Vancouver. I'm driving there tonight . . .'

Warmth flows back into my body. I remember to breathe. I glance at Nancy, realising she didn't mean to be cruel.

'Is your Mum OK?' I ask, walking back towards the cabin beside her, glad that she is holding the dog between us and the other one has run off somewhere. Again she doesn't seem to register the question.

'It took a week! That damn letter took a week to get here, my Dad wrote me from Vancouver the day it happened. Jim just brought me the letter but he has to charge the battery on the truck. Otherwise I can't drive all that way . . .'

She's close to tears. Gently, I try again to ask her about her mother and she finally hears the question and nods, shortly.

'I don't know. I – a car hit her as she was turning onto the freeway. I don't know. It's so – frustrating! I have to wait hours before I make the drive.'

We've reached the cabin. Frances is upstairs, with Clay and Katie and from the squeals and yells, she's obviously fine.

'I'm sorry, Nancy. Can I get you anything? You must be – very shocked. Do you need a coffee, or something?'

Nancy slumps onto the sofa, nods at the coffee pot, smiles weakly at me and I see she is struggling to talk to me, to remember my existence.

'It's just so frustrating, at times, you know? Living here. No telephone and all of that. Mom might be – it might be – and the only way I get to find out is when the men drop by with a letter . . .'

I pour her a coffee, black with one spoonful of honey, and I'm concentrating on this, and noticing a blue jay through the kitchen window, pecking at the dog's bowl on the grass outside, and it is a while before the impact of what she just said sinks in. But when it does I'm back to square one, back to the panic of a moment ago, when I thought something terrible had happened. I realise that it has.

'The men brought you the letter? You mean, do you mean, Mick and Jim?'

'Jim didn't know what was in the letter. They finished work around five. It's pay day, you know. They were about to go have a drink, over at Sam's. When I read the letter,

Jim said he'd take the battery and fix up the truck so I can drive there later tonight. They went to Joe's in Goldtown. He can charge it up. Joe has electricity.'

She's obsessed with details about the truck, the battery. I keep wanting to rewind her, go back to the bit about the men turning up.

'Was Mick with him?' I ask.

'Thanks,' Nancy accepts the coffee, sips it, stares at the pan of water on her barrel stove.

'Was Mick with him?' I ask again, more insistently this time. The dread flooding through me makes the words sharp, I feel like shaking her.

'Yes,' she replies. She sounds surprised, perhaps at the tone of my voice. She hasn't cottoned on then. 'Mick had to give Jim a lift from the valley up here. Our truck is in Goldtown, with a flat battery.' Now it's her turn to sound exasperated with me, with my inability to grasp the problem. She has no truck. She wants to drive to Vancouver but the truck has a flat battery.

I sit down beside her, the hand holding the coffee cup is shaking. The children seem very quiet all of a sudden. No dogs barking. No shouting.

'Did Mick see Frances?' I ask.

'Yes.'

'Did he ask what she was doing here?'

'Yeah. I said you needed a break. I told him you'd probably gone for a walk.'

So she didn't buy the shopping story. She looks worriedly at me, the arched eyebrows more exaggerated than ever, like two enormous question-marks over each eye.

'Have I said something wrong?'

I take a gulp of scalding coffee. My mouth is dry. I don't know how to reply, what I could possibly say to Nancy to explain the chattering in my teeth, the shaking hands around the coffee cup, the drumming in my ribcage.

'Oh God. I don't know,' I manage, eventually. 'Where did Mick go? What did they do after that?'

'I think they drove over to yours, then Mick promised to give Jim a lift downtown. They're probably drinking at Sam's. I don't expect they'll be back for a while. I'm sorry honey, if I said the wrong thing.'

She's shaking her head, I can tell she doesn't understand, but from my reaction, she clearly knows that something is wrong.

'I'd better get Frances and go back. I suppose I'd better take Frances and go back. I should – um – get Frances now and . . .'

I stand at the bottom of the ladder, shouting up to Frances, to come on now and get Sindy and let's go home. Nancy is still sitting stiffly on the sofa. The city clothes – the old-fashioned skirt and the brushed hair – transform her. No longer the capable mother, the hippy with the gorgeous kids and the wilderness home and the dogs and the faith and the home-made biscuits; she's just Nancy now. Married to an alcoholic, with no electricity and a mother in hospital and a truck with a flat battery. I long to apologise for something, for envying her, perhaps, but that's not quite it. Longing for her would be more accurate. Longing, as ever, for someone stronger than me. A Cherie-Rose who could fight back.

Frances appears at the top of the stairs, dressed only in a T-shirt and with a face smeared with kool-aid. I take a deep breath, trying to calm myself, gather myself.

Maybe it'll be all right, maybe Mick won't be suspicious, maybe I've got away with it this time. And there's not going to be another.

'It's OK,' I force myself to say to Nancy. 'I hope your Mum is fine. Drive safely, this evening. And thanks, thanks a lot for having Frances . . .'

I buckle up the straps on the blue jelly shoes, while Frances, predictably, bats me on the head with the Sindy.

## 30

Mick comes back far later than I expect. Frances is upstairs fast asleep, after the hours I have been sitting here, rocking her, burying my face in her smoke-scented hair, rocking and waiting and listening. I know the minute the truck tyres slur over the stones outside that he is drunk.

I'm sitting with the lamp on and two candles lit and the fire crackling. The instant he walks in I feel the danger of this. Fire. I long to leap up and blow the candles out, throw water everywhere, I actually look around for the water container as the door opens with its usual abrupt jolt and gust of cool air.

'Had a nice day, darling?' he says, in a voice so dangerous, so clogged with fury, I wonder why I never heard that voice before.

There's no time to think, anything. I leap up. I don't even try to pretend. I'm terrified.

'Mick, what is it?'

'You're such a bitch.' He stands as close as he could ever be without being inside me, eclipsing me completely. He is shaking, trembling from head to toe like a flame.

Oh my god oh my god oh my god oh my god oh my god ohmygod

'Shut up you mad bitch. What's the matter with you? I know what you've been up to, I'm not fucking stupid—'

'I don't know what you're talking about.'

Of course I do, I do, why am I saying this? I'm only trying to play for time, I don't want to lie to Mick, I want to talk about it, like other couples, but this thought brings me up short, it's breathtakingly ridiculous. Talk things through! When am I going to understand? The things I've glimpsed, believed he would never do, what if I'm wrong? What if, all along, I should have trusted my fear?

A white light is blanking him out. He is so aflame that I can barely see him – or perhaps I'm the one aflame? Where are my glasses? I can't see anything, I can only feel, feel at this pitch, this heat.

Mick is making this strange noise, almost wailing, low and long and he seems not to know that he is doing it. He breaks off to say, 'You've been with him, haven't you? That bastard Ryan. Why else would you leave Frankie with Nancy? Where else would you be? I came back here you know, with Jim. I thought you might be here. I trusted you . . .' Then he buries his face in his hands and slumps towards the wall of the cabin. I'm sick with guilt now at the sight of him. The rawness, the thing Mick has teased and tantalised me with from the start; his vulnerability, his pain, his terrible need of me.

I make a move, a tiny move, I'm about to move towards him – even now, I want to put my arms around him – when he pulls his hands away from his face and instead, in an odd, childish gesture – almost a hug – he throws himself at me. The force of his weight against me – his chest against mine – makes my knees fold. I stagger back against the sofa, but I manage to spring up instantly, grabbing the heavy torch from the floor beside me and holding it in front of me, brandishing it.

'Don't threaten me,' he sneers, his voice thick with beer, and sarcasm, swaying towards me.

'I – I'm not. I'm just – Mick, you promised.'

I want him to see me. Why can't he see me, understand

that it's me, Rita, I love him, I'm a good person, I'm frightened.

'Shut up! Shut up!' he's screaming, he seems in a worse panic than I am, or is that someone else screaming? Suddenly he has his hands around my throat and the torch is crushed against my body. His blue eyes are inches from mine and his fingers are burning into my neck. I am going to burst right out of this skin like a hot slice of toast leaping from the toaster. He's going to do it, what he's wanted all along, squeeze me through his fingers to where he thinks I should be; not six foot under, not heaven or hell but somewhere far, far worse; where everyone who loves him is; lost, obliterated, nowhere at all. And that's precisely where I've wanted to be.

Mick is shaking me. Rage is rising in me, crackling through my veins. His hands are still around my throat but there is a strength, beginning in my stomach and it is an animal strength, like labour; those long hours of Frances's birth where I found more and more strength, I kept bringing it forward, one wave after another and here it is again. He is drunk after all. I can feel the beer on my face, and the sloppiness in him. If we were making love right now, that's how it would be. Sloppy, fluid, heavy. My arms grow strong as branches. My hands clutch around the torch, feeling it press into my ribcage. I struggle to lift the torch clamped between us and then in an abrupt movement my arm is free and I bring it swinging round from the outside, with a crash aimed badly at Mick's head. The second finds its mark more readily. It is a light blow. It makes hardly a sound. He closes his eyes. I feel the strength flow out of his fingers. His body is turning to water, trickling into the cabin floor. Fire pours out of me, roars in my ears.

# 31

I wake Frances gently, shaking her sweaty shoulder until her eyes open and the cross little face forms. 'Out,' she demands. I lift her out of the cot, dress her hurriedly. I grab a bag from under the bed, swinging the torch around to light up things to stuff into it; passport, the money order from Carole, some books, some clothes. Essentials. The rest has to stay and as I'm bundling Frances down the steps, her small heartbeat pounding against mine, I'm glancing round at the cabin, thinking: What about that? I wish I could take that . . .

The keys to the truck are on the floor where they fell from Mick's pocket. I venture as close as I dare, capturing them in a saucer of torch-light and struggling to pick them up with Frances in one arm, the bag in the other. Mick is lying on the floor, where I've thrown a blanket over him. His body is a grey lumpen presence in the corner of my eye. I mustn't look. All I have to do is not look at him. I'm wearing my glasses, but it's fine, I can manage it, I still have the knack. I'm good at not looking.

I wish I could say goodbye. To Ryan. To Mount Coyote . . . I don't know. Whoever. But we'd better move fast. God, I hope Nancy hasn't gone yet. Frances makes no sound as I push against the cabin door. She's half asleep. The door opens noisily and Mick gives a sudden moan inside the cabin. A drunken moan. Mick isn't dead. What he is is dead-drunk.

The petrol has left my veins, I'm poured out. Everything I feared, everything I thought was outside is inside me. All that darkness, the twigs snapping. Inside.

The moonlight is milky, faint but just enough, combined with the small bouncing pool from the torch as we run to the truck. An owl gives a low, rolling hoot, ravelling like wool around the forest.

'Come on, Frankie,' I whisper, setting her down on the ground while I panic for a moment, feeling for the keys I just picked up. 'It's OK,' I mutter to her, to soothe myself, 'Here's Sindy. No time for breakfast, I'll get you something at a gas station. We're going to Nancy's. Going in Nancy's truck. All the way to Vancouver. Nice journey. We're going on an aeroplane.'

Trembling in the chilly night air, I find the keys and gingerly open the truck door, throw the bag on the passenger seat and strap Frances into her baby-seat. Her hand is in my hair, tightening with a handful, ready to pull.

'No, Frances,' I say, gently untangling her hand. 'Be kind to me. That hurts.'

The fingers retain their clasp, but she doesn't pull. She allows me to open her hand and release my hair, easing my head away as if I was withdrawing from the jaws of a lion. 'Thank you. Good girl,' I whisper to her. She puts a stubby forefinger to my cheek and tears flow over it.

I have the key in my hand. I'm shaking and trying to shine the torch in the place where the key turns and everything is smeary and I'm remembering the strangest thing. It doesn't seem relevant to anything. Mum, Dan, Billy, Tony and me. Leaving the house one morning in winter on the way to school. Mum in a big raincoat, in a flap as usual, locking up the new house and rushing down the drive. She slips. She falls flying, flat on her back in the middle of the street and we all turn round and stare at her. None of us dare to laugh. I don't know if the others are even thinking of it, I know I'm not. My lovely Mum with her long hair brushing the pavement, the new raincoat she got from the catalogue brown and mucky on the back and now she is standing up brushing at it, fighting tears and telling us to hurry up, she hasn't got all day . . .

It's the sight of her lying there. The pain I feel on her behalf. The humiliation, annoyance. The need to help her up, to have her upright, taking us to school, not flapping on the street like a piece of paper.

'Come on, Rita, I'm OK, what's the matter with you?' she says gruffly, producing a tissue from her pocket to scrub at the mark, twisting the back of the coat round to look at it, telling my brothers – now giggling, now the crisis has passed – to get a move on. I'm weeping stupidly and I keep saying to her: 'Your lovely coat, your new coat, you love that coat.' But what I really mean is: I don't want you to be hurt. I can't bear to see you fall down.

When I think of the ways in which Frances has seen me hurt, my heart twists. She has seen me kicked on the floor like a dog. She has seen me screaming, terrified, and trying to pretend I'm not. I thought she didn't love me, loved Mick best, needed a father more than I needed to be free of Mick. I think I was wrong. She needs what every child needs. She needs to be allowed to love her mother, to believe her mother is the best in the world, at least for a time. Mick and I have been preventing that.

I can't risk allowing Frances to say goodbye to Mick and she might never forgive me. I've dreaded that . . . Frances never forgiving me. Mick never forgave Cherie-Rose. I never forgave my father. Staying, leaving, we never forgive our parents for something. But I intend to keep my promise to Frances. One of the three of us has to be the adult here, weigh up the real or imagined danger, trust the shit we know we're in. And that job has landed on me.

If I can get this engine started without it waking him,

without him running out here, we're safe. I can't bring myself to turn the key. What if it doesn't start? Every nerve in my body has turned to liquid. All those nights Mick didn't hear the coyote. All those times when Frances's crying didn't disturb him. He's a heavy sleeper, even sober. If Nancy has left for Vancouver already, I can drive down the mountain, abandon the truck and hitch a lift to Vancouver. This truck is automatic. I've driven in pitch-black through a mountain forest before now. I've driven between ours and Nancy's. All I have to do is turn the key and put the truck into drive.

I lean back against the seat and take a deep breath. Then I open the truck door and step outside. I can't leave. In the splashes of torch-light outside I spot a few remaining moths fluttering around the tips of the nearest Ponderosas. Bending down, I pick up a pine cone and know it belongs to a Douglas Fir, feeling each scale on the cone covered by a finer, forked scale. I hold it in one hand and with the other hand whirl the torch over everything; the cabin, the dying Nootka rose, the salmonberry bushes, the rocks, the tree-stumps. I'll never see any of it again.

There was a forest fire here about fifty years ago. That's why the trees are so thin and spaced out, that's why there are no really big ones, and so many Lodgepole pine. Lodgepole favour land after a fire. So do certain plants; fireweed for instance. Some things grow back, some things never do. Maybe a fire right now would get rid of the pine-beetle, the moths; this might be what our land needs more than anything. But there's another way of looking at it. Nancy says the pine-beetle attack weakened trees. Trees weakened by fire. Whether savage fires are healing, cleansing or whether they devastate beyond repair, leave a site forever vulnerable, altered, damaged, what do I know?

'Dwink!' Frances pipes up, from inside the truck. I switch

off the torch and her fluffy hair glows softly in the moonlight like white gold. I climb back in beside her, closing
the door gently. I turn the key and the engine growls
into life.

# The Passion of Alice
## STEPHANIE GRANT

'One of the most amazing aspects . . . is that although the protagonist is an anorexic woman struggling with her sexuality while in a mental hospital, the novel itself is not an "anorexic's story" a "sexual identity story" or even a "mental illness story." It is simply a smart, funny wonderful book that will contain truth for every reader . . . a stunner of a first novel'
*Los Angeles Times*

'A compelling first novel . . . Subtle and ironic . . . Grant writes with such dry perception and quick-fire scene changes that her material stimulates rather than depresses'
*Times Literary Supplement*

'An utterly convincing, enthralling story of women and hunger . . . it kept me up until two o'clock in the morning'
*Emma Donoghue*

'A fascinating, unsentimental look at eating disorders . . . compelling, erotic, melancholy and darkly funny all at once'
*Gay Times*

'A raw book of great power'
*Village Voice*

∫

SCEPTRE

# Decorations in a Ruined Cemetery

## JOHN GREGORY BROWN

### Winner of the Steinbeck Award

'Set in New Orleans, *Decorations in a Ruined Cemetery*
begins on the day that the Lake Pontchartrain
Causeway collapsed. One car plunges into the water
– its driver is later retrieved "bloated like a whale" –
and all the other Sunday travellers must turn back.
Among them is Thomas Eagen, who that morning had
packed his belongings and his 12-year-old twins into
his car and left his wife to head for a new start in his
childhood home. But, as the bridge crumbles, all his
plans go with it and, it seems to his daughter, it is
then that the whole Eagen world is thrown off-balance
. . . an historical family saga of miscegenation and
misery, of the depths of racism and the thickness of
blood . . . Moving, wise and wonderful'
*The Times*

'Reading it is to rush willingly and excitedly across a
minefield, waiting for blasts of revelation . . . Brown is
a dancing funambulist of a writer who breathtakingly
shifts back and forth between events . . . a masterpiece'
*New Statesman and Society*

'A beautiful novel . . . Artistry like this is unclassifiable'
*The New York Times Book Review*

'Stunning . . . Compassionate and profound
*The Chicago Tribune*

∫

SCEPTRE